B. P. Pratten

The Fairy World

With 68 colored engravings

B. P. Pratten

The Fairy World
With 68 colored engravings

ISBN/EAN: 9783337240530

Printed in Europe, USA, Canada, Australia, Japan

Cover: Foto ©Andreas Hilbeck / pixelio.de

More available books at **www.hansebooks.com**

THE

FAIRY WORLD.

WITH 68 COLORED ENGRAVINGS.

FISHER & BROTHER,

No. 12 NORTH SIXTH ST., PHILADELPHIA.

The Fair One with Golden Locks.

THERE was once a princess who had such a beautiful head of hair, streaming down in curls to her feet, and brilliant as a sunbeam, that she was universally called the Fair One with Golden Locks. A neighbouring king, having heard a great deal of her beauty, fell in love with her upon hearsay, and sent an ambassador with a magnificent suite to ask her in marriage, bidding him be sure and not fail to bring the princess home with him. The ambassador did his best to fulfil the king's commands, and made as fair a speech as he could to persuade the lady; but either she was not in a good temper that day, or his eloquence failed to move her, for she answered, that she thanked the king, but had no mind to marry. So the ambassador returned home with all the presents he had brought, as the princess would not accept any thing of a suitor whom she refused, much to the grief of the king, who had made the most splendid preparations to receive her, never doubting but what she would come.

Now, there happened to be at court a very handsome young man, named Avenant, who observed, that had he been sent to the Fair One with Golden Locks, he would certainly have persuaded her to come; whereupon some ill-natured persons, who were jeal-

ous of the favour he enjoyed, repeated his words to the king, as though he had meant to boast that, being handsomer than his majesty, the princess would certainly have followed him. This threw the king into

4

such a rage, that he ordered poor Avenant to be
thrown into a dungeon, where he had nothing but
straw to lie upon, and where he would have died of
exhaustion had it not been for a little spring that
welled forth at the foot of the tower in which he
was confined. One day, when he felt as if he were
near his end, he could not help exclaiming, "What
have I done? and what can have hardened the
king's heart against the most faithful of all his subjects?" It chanced that the king passed by just as
he uttered these words, and, being melted by his
former favourite's grief, he ordered the prison-door
to be opened, and bid him come forth. Avenant
fell at his feet, entreating to know the cause of his
disgrace. "Did you not make game both of myself
and my ambassador?" said the king; "and did you
not boast that had I sent you to the Fair One with
Golden Locks, you would have prevailed on her to
return with you?" "True, sire," replied Avenant;
"for I should have set forth all your great qualities
so irresistibly, that I am certain she could not have
said nay. Methinks there is no treason in that."
The king was so convinced of his innocence, that
he straightway released Avenant from prison and

5

brought him back to the palace. After having given him a good supper, the king took him into his cabinet, and confessed to him that he was still so in love with the Fair One with Golden Locks, that he had a great mind to send him to obtain her hand, and meant to prepare a splendid equipage befitting the ambassador of a great nation. But Avenant said, "That is not necessary. Only give me a good horse, and the necessary credentials, and I will set off to-morrow."

On the following morning Avenant left the court, and set out alone on his journey, thinking as he went of all the fine things he should say to the princess, and stopping ever and anon, when any pretty conceit came into his head, to jot it down on his tablets. One day as he halted for this purpose in a lovely meadow by the side of a rivulet, he perceived a large golden carp, that lay gasping upon the grass, having jumped so high to snap at the flies that she had overreached herself, and was unable to get back into the water. Avenant took pity on her, and, gently lifting her up, restored her to her native element. The carp took a plunge to refresh herself, then, reappearing on the surface, she said, "Thanks, Avenant, for saving my life. I will do you a good turn if

6

ever I can." So saying, she dived back into the water, leaving Avenant greatly surprised at her civility.

Another time, he saw a crow closely pursued by a

large eagle, when, thinking it would be a shame not to defend the weak against the strong, he let fly an arrow that brought the cruel bird of prey to the ground, while the crow perched upon a tree in great delight, crying, "It was very generous of you, Avenant, to help a poor crow like me. But I will prove grateful, and do you a good turn whenever I can."

Avenant was pleased with the crow's good feelings, and continued his journey; when, some days after, as he crossed a thick wood, he heard an owl hooting, as if in great distress. After looking about him on all sides, Avenant found the poor owl had got entangled in a net. He soon cut the meshes, and set him free. The owl soared aloft, then, wheeling back, cried, "Avenant, I was caught, and should have been killed without your help. But I am grateful, and will do you a good turn when I can."

Such were the principal adventures that befell Avenant on his journey. When, at last, he reached the capital where resided the Fair One with Golden Locks, it appeared so magnificent that he thought he should be lucky indeed if he could persuade her to leave such wonders to come and marry the king his master. He, however, determined to do his best: so, having put on a brocaded dress, with a richly-embroidered scarf, and hung round his neck a small basket, containing a beautiful little dog he had bought on the road, he asked for admittance at the palace-gate with such graceful dignity that the guards all bowed respectfully, and the attendants ran to announce the arrival of another ambassador, named Avenant, from the king her neighbour.

The princess bid her women fetch the blue brocaded satin gown, and dress her hair with fresh wreaths of flowers; and when her toilet was completed, she entered her audience-chamber, where Avenant was waiting for her. Though dazzled at the sight of her rare beauty, he nevertheless delivered an eloquent harangue, which he wound up by entreating the princess not to give him the pain of returning without her. "Gentle Avenant," replied she, "your speech is fair; but you must know that a month ago I let fall into the river a ring that I value above my kingdom, and I made a vow, at the time, that I would never listen to a marriage-proposal from anybody, unless his ambassador recovered my lost treasure. So, you see, were you to talk till doomsday, you could not shake my determination."

Avenant went to bed supperless that night; nor could he close his eyes for a long while, but kept lamenting that the princess required impossible things to put him off the suit he had undertaken. But his little dog Cabriole bid him be of good cheer, as for-

tune would no doubt favour him; and, though Avenant did not much rely on his good luck, he at length fell asleep from sheer exhaustion.

The next morning Cabriole woke up his master,

10

who dressed himself and went to take a walk. His feet insensibly carried him to the river-side, when he heard a voice calling out, "Avenant! Avenant!" He looked about him, but, seeing no one, was proceeding on his way, when Cabriole, who was looking at the water, cried, "Why, master, as I'm alive, it is a golden carp that is hailing you." Upon which the carp approached, saying, "You saved my life in the meadow, and I promised to be grateful. So here is the ring you are seeking for, gentle Avenant."

He then hastened to the palace, and, requesting an audience of the princess, he presented her the ring, and asked whether she had any objection now to marry his master. On seeing her ring she was greatly amazed; but, being intent on putting him off once more, she replied, "Since you are so ready to fulfil my behests, most gracious Avenant, I pray you do me another service, without which I cannot marry. There lives not far from here a giant named Galifron, who has threatened to ravage my kingdom unless I grant him my hand. He is daily killing and eating my subjects; and if you want to win my good graces on your master's behalf, you must bring me the giant's head."

11

Avenant was taken somewhat aback at this proposal; yet, after a few moments' reflection, he said,
"Well, madam, I am ready to fight Galifron; and,
though I may not conquer, I can, at least, die the
death of a hero." The princess, who had never expected Avenant would consent, now sought to dis-
suade him from so rash an attempt; but all she could
say proved vain; and, having equipped himself for
the fight, he mounted his horse and departed.

As he approached Galifron's castle, he found the
road strewed with the bones and carcasses of those
whom he had devoured or torn to pieces; and presently the giant emerged from the wood, when, seeing
Avenant with his sword drawn, he ran at him with
his iron club, and would have killed him on the spot,
had not a crow come and pecked at his eyes, and
made the blood stream down his face; so that, while
he aimed his blows at random, Avenant plunged his
sword up to the hilt into his heart. Avenant then
cut off his head, and the crow perched on a tree,
saying, "I have not forgotten how you saved my
life by killing the eagle. I promised to do you a
good turn, and I have kept my word." "In truth,
I am greatly beholden to you, master crow," quoth
12

Avenant, as he mounted his horse and rode off with Galifron's head.

When he reached the city, the inhabitants gathered round him, and accompanied him with loud cheers

to the palace. The princess, who had trembled for his safety, was delighted to see him return. "Now, madam," said Avenant, "I think you have no excuse left for not marrying my liege lord." "Yes, indeed I have," answered she; "and I shall still refuse him unless you procure me some water from the fountain of beauty. This water lies in a grotto guarded by two dragons. Inside the grotto is a large hole, full of toads and serpents, by which you descend to a small cellar containing the spring. Whoever washes her face with this water retains her beauty, if already beautiful, or becomes beautiful, though ever so ugly. It makes the young remain young, and the old become young again. So you see, Avenant, I cannot leave my kingdom without carrying some of this water away with me." "Methinks, madam," observed Avenant, "you are far too beautiful to need any such water ; but, as you seek the death of your humble servant, I must go and die."

Accordingly, Avenant set out with his faithful little dog, and at last reached a high mountain, from the top of which he perceived a rock as black as ink, whence issued clouds of smoke. Presently, out came a green and yellow dragon, whose eyes and nostrils were pouring forth fire, and whose tail had at least a hundred coils. Avenant drew his sword, and, taking out a phial given him by the Fair One with Golden Locks, said to Cabriole, "I shall never be able to reach the water: so, when I am killed, fill this phial with my blood, and take it to the princess, that she may

14

see what she has cost me, and then go and inform
the king, my master, of the fate that has befallen me."
While he was speaking, a voice called out, "Avenant!
Avenant!" and he perceived an owl in the hollow of
a tree, who said, "You freed me from the bird-
catcher's net, and I promised to do you a good turn.
So give me your phial, and I will go and fetch the
water of beauty." And away flew the owl, who,
knowing all the turnings and windings of the grotto,
soon returned, bearing back his prize. After thanking the owl, Avenant went back to the palace, where
he presented the bottle to the princess, who agreed
to set out with him for his master's kingdom.

On reaching the capital, the king came forth to
meet the Fair One with Golden Locks, and made her
the most sumptuous presents. They were then married, amid great festivities and rejoicings; but the
queen, who loved Avenant in her heart, could not
forbear incessantly reminding the king that had it
not been for Avenant she would never have come.
So it happened that some meddling bodies went
and told the king that she preferred Avenant to
himself, when he became so jealous that he ordered
his faithful subject to be thrown into prison. When

15

the Fair One with Golden Locks heard of his disgrace, she implored the king to release him; but the more she entreated, the more obstinately his

majesty refused. The king now imagined that his wife perhaps did not think him handsome enough: so he had a mind to try the effects of washing his face with the water of beauty. Accordingly, one

16

night he took the phial from off the mantel-piece in
the queen's bedchamber, and rubbed his face well
before he went to bed. But, unfortunately, a short
time previous the phial had been broken by one
of the maids, as she was dusting, and, to avoid a
scolding, she had replaced it by a phial which she
found in the king's cabinet, containing a wash similar in appearance, but deadly in its effects. The
king went to sleep, and died. Cabriole ran to his
master to tell him the news, when Avenant bid him
go and remind the queen of the poor prisoner. So
Cabriole slipped in among the crowd of courtiers
who had assembled on the king's death, and whis-
pered to her majesty, "Do not forget poor Avenant."
The queen then called to mind all he had suffered on
her account, and, hastening to the tower, she took off
his chains with her own white hands, and throwing
the royal mantle over his shoulders, and placing a
gold crown on his head, she said, "I choose you for
my husband, Avenant, and you shall be king."
Everybody was delighted at her choice, the wedding
was the grandest ever seen, and the Fair One with
Golden Locks, and her faithful Avenant, lived hap-
pily to a good old age.

The Little Fisher-Boy.

Upon a small and lonely island in the wide ocean there once lived a poor old fisherman, who supported his family by his honest industry. As he was a very quiet, contented man, he lived on the very best terms with the numerous nixes, who often resorted to this solitary spot in preference to the more frequented lands on the sea-shore. They would even occasionally help him at his work, and show him where the best fishes were to be found, and sometimes would fling a rare one into his boat as he was going home. They warned him, too, of coming storms, and pointed out shoals and quicksands, and, in short, lightened his toils so effectually that, in spite of his advanced age, he performed his daily labours with very little fatigue. In return for all this kindness, the fisherman, on his part, never intruded on their favourite haunts; and when he sailed to the nearest city to dispose of the rich produce of his day's fishing, he frequently

13.

brought them back presents of chains, or rings, or
little silver bells, in all of which trinkets the nixes
take great delight. As the parents were on such a
friendly footing with the inhabitants of the deep,
the children on both sides were mutually allowed
to grow intimate with each other; and it was a
pretty sight to see the fisherman's little boys and
girls frolicking with the agile nixes along the shore,
or playing a thousand tricks with their watery play-
mates when they put out to sea in their skiff. But
the fisherman's eldest son, Haldan, had more especially formed a closer friendship with one little nix,
who had once saved him from drowning when his
fragile boat had been upset by a gale of wind.
And these two would often leave their noisier companions, and retire into a lonely little creek, where
they could play and talk quietly together, half concealed by the sea-weeds, and beneath the shade of
overhanging rocks. Haldan used to bring his dear
little Goldtail — as his brothers and sisters nick-
named her, on account of her beautiful golden
scales—the pretty flowers he had gathered in the
meadows or on the mountain; while Goldtail, in
return, would present him with a large shell con-

taining costly pearls and sprigs of coral. Each was
so delighted with the other's gifts that they would
adorn themselves with their mutual presents, and

play like two happy children. Sometimes, however, they were more thoughtful and serious; and
when Haldan told Goldtail all about the cottage
where they lived, and the little garden with its
20

trim flowers, and the games he played with other children, or described the grand, large city, whither his father had often taken him, with its many, many inhabitants, its majestic buildings and glittering shops, the little nix would sigh and grow sad, and scarcely be able to repress a bitter tear, as she exclaimed, "Oh, how I wish I might go and live with you! It must be so fair to dwell on the green, sunny earth!"

And then she looked down sorrowfully on her glittering tail, which all her sisters so greatly envied. Haldan, too, would sigh, and embrace his little playmate, saying, "Ay! if that could but be, how we would love one another!"

Then Goldtail would repeat to him what she had heard from her good old aunt Graytail, namely, that she might be changed to a human shape; provided any kind-hearted mortal would shed his blood to save her from death. After that, her scales would fall, and she would become like any other human being; only she must never so much as touch sea-water, or she would instantly be changed back again to her pristine form. But these conversations only made the poor children grow still sadder,—as they

21

saw no possibility of fulfilling such conditions; for though Haldan pricked his arm, and let the blood drop upon Goldtail, it proved of no avail, and she remained just the same as before.

One day, as they sat talking of their favourite topic, and were very much out of heart, they suddenly heard the rustling of a pair of mighty wings above their heads, and, before they could collect their thoughts, a formidable eagle had pounced upon Goldtail, and was about to carry her off in his claws, when Haldan suddenly seized a stick that had been cast upon the shore by chance, and, attacking the eagle with a kind of desperate courage, forced him to relinquish his hold. The infuriated bird now turned round upon the little boy, and struck the club out of his hands with a flap of his strong wings, and tore his flesh with his sharp beak, and seized him in his claws to fly away with him, in spite of Goldtail's cries for help. The poor little nix could only wring her hands in helpless despair, as the eagle slowly soared upwards with his prize. But, luckily, Haldan's arms had remained free, and no sooner did the smarting of his wounds arouse him from his stupor than he

22

seized convulsively upon the eagle's throat, and strangled him, before he had flown very high, so that both fell down together into the sea.

When Haldan had recovered from the stunning effects of his fall, he found himself on the shore in the arms of Goldtail, who was tenderly washing and binding up his wounds. And—oh, wonder of

wonders!—a second glance at his playmate showed
him that she had lost her golden tail, and was now
like one of his own little sisters. In the fulness
of their joy, they fell upon each other's neck, as
though they had met again after a long separa-
tion; and Haldan forgot his wounds, and rose up to
take his little friend home and tell his family
what a piece of good luck had befallen him. But,
first of all, they fastened the eagle's feet to the
stick, and carried it on their shoulders, as they
gayly went along to the fisherman's cottage. They
had not proceeded far before they were met by
Haldan's youngest sister, who came running towards them as fast as she could, and told them
how the old nixes, having watched them, had com-
plained violently to their father about the loss of
their child, and how the latter had been compelled,
on their repeated demands, to promise to bind
Goldtail and fling her into the sea. The children
looked mournfully at each other, to think that their
dream of happiness should have vanished so soon;
and neither of them knew what to do or to advise.
At length they both exclaimed, in a breath, "No!
we will not part from one another;" and, taking

24

leave of Haldan's kind little sister, they turned back, and went to seek a safe retreat in a wild and distant part of the island, where they hoped to escape from their parents' pursuit.

After wandering for several days, they reached a thick forest, in which they found a grotto that seemed to offer a safe and agreeable abode. Near it ran a babbling stream, full of fish, while berries grew in countless thousands on the ground, and

3   25

the flocks of wild pigeons that had built their nests among the rocks would furnish them plenty of eggs for their nourishment. Here the children lived for a long time undiscovered, and played, and were as happy as the day was long, and used often to talk of future plans against they should be grown up. But their happiness was not to last. A fish that happened to escape from Haldan's net swam towards the sea, and betrayed the secret of their retreat, out of revenge, to one of the nixes. She immediately swam softly to the spot pointed out by the fish, and overheard the little hermits, as they sat unconsciously on the banks of the stream, warming themselves in the bright sunshine, and planning what they would do on the morrow, and where they had better fish, and how they should lay in a stock of provisions for the coming winter. After listening to their conversation, the nix swam back as noiselessly as she had come, and, calling her parents and brothers and sisters together, they all agreed to carry off Haldan when he would be fishing early next morning, as they had not the power to take their dear Goldtail by mere force. They, therefore, cautiously followed up the stream

26

that same night, in the moonshine, and the treacherous nix posted the strongest of the band in a hiding-place near the spot where she had heard Haldan would come to fish. Scarcely had dawn appeared in the horizon, and the birds awoke from their slumbers, when Haldan came along, singing as he went, in company with his Goldhair,—as he now called her; and, while he took out his fishing-tackle to set to work, she turned into a neighbouring path to gather berries. But no sooner had he set his foot in the water, in order to throw his net more conveniently, than the stalwart male nix stepped forth from behind the stump of a tree, where he lay hid, and, seizing hold of the boy, whom he flung across his shoulder, hastily swam down the stream; while the other nixes followed close upon him, so as to hinder the little captive from catching hold of a branch to save himself. His screams for help quickly brought Goldhair to the bank of the stream,—but, alas! only to see her friend's danger and to feel how powerless she was to assist him! In vain did she weep and implore, in language that would have moved a stone; the nixes remained inexorable, and bore their struggling prey to the ocean. Breathless and half distracted, Goldhair ran after them till she reached the sea-shore, when she started back in alarm, as a rising wave had nearly besprinkled her foot; for

she recollected with horror that she would again become a nix should she touch the waters of the sea. So she shuddered, and dared not advance a step farther, just as a piercing cry met her ears, and, on looking round, she perceived her faithful

23

Haldan being dragged down into the deep; when, losing sight of every thing but his safety, she recklessly plunged into the flood. Scarcely had she touched the water, when she felt herself trans-

formed; yet on she went, with the speed of lightning, and, tearing Haldan from the arms of these cruel robbers, she bore him to their favourite spot, which was close at hand. But it was too late; for

before she had laid her dear burden on the sea-
shore, life was already extinct!

> To winds and waves she tells her grief,
>   And asks them to restore his breath;
> But winds nor waves can give relief,
>   Nor tears can soften ruthless death.
>
> She digs his grave within the deep,
>   Mid pearls and gems, in caverns dim;
> And, soon as he is laid to sleep,
>   She, dying, sings his funeral hymn.

Jack and the Bean-Stalk.

In the days of King Alfred there lived, in a remote village in England, a poor widow, whose son was so spoiled by over-indulgence that he was the idlest and most careless boy in the whole parish. These two faults, together with his reckless extravagance, had brought his mother to the very brink of ruin; so that at length, when there was not a crust of bread left in the house, she told Jack, with tears in her eyes, that her cow must now be sold, to prevent their starving. Jack felt sorry to see his mother so dejected, and promised, if she would trust him to drive the cow to the next village, he would sell her to the best advantage. The mother, believing in her son's sudden reform, allowed him to set out with the cow, upon whose back the lazy fellow rode astride; but he had not reached half-way to the village before he met a butcher, who was carrying some curious-looking beans in his hat. While Jack was eyeing the beans, the butcher eyed the cow, and, feeling pretty sure of making a good bargain with such a

careless fellow, he inquired whether he would exchange the cow for the pretty beans in his hat.

Jack was so delighted at the proposal that he

agreed to it in a moment, and, jumping down, ran
back in breathless haste to tell his mother what he
had done, expecting that she would be as much

pleased as himself. When the poor widow heard
of this crowning piece of folly and carelessness, her
despair and exasperation were such that she flung
the beans about in all directions, and both mother
and son went supperless to bed.

Jack woke early next morning, when, perceiving
his window darkened by a foliage he had never seen
before, he ran down into the garden, and found that
the beans had taken root during the night, and
sprung up to such an amazing height as to form a
kind of natural ladder, the top of which was lost in
the clouds. He immediately formed the determination of climbing up it, and this, in spite of all his
mother's remonstrances, he speedily proceeded to
do.

Jack climbed and climbed for several hours, and
was beginning to get quite exhausted, when at length
he reached the top of the bean-stalk, and found himself in a strange land, where not a tree or a shrub,
and still less a house or a living creature, were to be
seen. He now bitterly repented his disobedience,
and began to fear he should die of hunger before he
could get down again, when he suddenly perceived
a young and beautiful woman hovering over him.

33

While he was wondering at this apparition, the fair
stranger inquired how he came there.

Jack told the story of the bean-stalk; and then
she asked him whether he recollected his father, to

which the little fellow replied that he did not, and
that whenever he asked his mother about him she
would burst into tears, and he dared not question

her any further. The lady then said, "You shall hear the whole story; but first promise me solemnly to do what I command, for I am a fairy, and, should you fail to keep your word, you will be punished by death."

Jack, somewhat alarmed, promised to fulfil her injunctions faithfully, when she proceeded, thus:—

"Your father, as wealthy as he was benevolent, not only made it a rule never to let a day pass by without doing good to some one, but once a week kept open house, and invited to his table all those who had been reduced from better circumstances to a state of penury. Of course, he was known and beloved for miles around, when the fame of his good deeds reached the ears of a giant, who, being both envious and wicked, determined to enrich himself by effecting your father's ruin. The giant came with his wife into your father's neighbourhood, and, pretending to have lost all his property by an earthquake, was kindly received by your parents. One day that there blew a tremendous gale along the seashore, not far from which stood your father's house, the giant, on looking through a telescope, discovered some ships in distress, when he hastened to your

35

father, and entreated him to send all the servants he
could spare to assist the sufferers, well knowing that
such an appeal would be quickly responded to. Sure
enough, all the servants were despatched in a moment, with the exception of your nurse and the
porter, when the giant fell upon your unfortunate
parent and stabbed him to the heart. He next mur-
dered the two servants, and was going to sacrifice
your mother and yourself, then an infant three
months old, when the unhappy lady, fell at his feet,
entreating him to spare your life and hers,—a boon
she at last obtained, by taking a solemn oath never
to reveal your father's story to you. She then fled
with frantic haste, while the giant, repenting of his
mercy, would have pursued her, had he not been
anxious to gather up your father's treasures, set fire
to the house, and escape with his wife before the
return of the servants. Your poor mother wandered for miles, till at last she settled in the cottage
where you were brought up; and it is to make good
her wrongs that I caused you to be tempted to purchase the beans, and the bean-stalk to shoot up so
wonderfully, to give you an opportunity of punishing
the giant; for unless you persist in revenging your

father's death, you will never know happiness. Remember, you have full liberty to seize on the giant's possessions, for they are yours by right; but mind you do not betray to your mother that you are acquainted with the secret of your birth till we meet again.. Now go,—you will soon reach your enemy's residence; and bear in mind that so long as you obey my orders my vigilance will guard you."

The fairy then vanished, and Jack pursued his journey till sunset, when he reached a large mansion, and, seeing a woman at the door, he requested her to give him a crust of bread and a night's lodging.

"Alas!" said she, "I dare not! For my husband is a mighty giant, who delights in eating human flesh, and is now gone out in search of some: so you would not be safe for a moment in our house."

Terrified as Jack was, still he begged the good woman just to take him in for that night only, and hide him as best she could,—which, being naturally compassionate, she consented to do. They then entered a fine large hall, magnificently decorated, and went through a suite of rooms all equally splendid, though desolate-looking enough, till they reached a long gallery, dimly lighted, but where Jack could

4

just manage to see an iron grating that ran along one whole side, forming a dungeon, from whence proceeded the lamentations of the unhappy victims destined to appease the giant's voracious hunger. Jack's blood half curdled at the sound, and he began to doubt whether the good woman had not caught him in a trap. They emerged, however, into a spacious kitchen, where she laid a plentiful supper before him: so he forgot his fears, and was beginning to eat heartily, when a thundering rap at the door made the very house shake. The giant's wife had only time to hide Jack in the oven, and flew to let her husband in.

"I smell fresh meat!" said he, on entering.

"Oh!" replied she, "it is only the inmates of the dungeon." So he walked in grumbling, while Jack, more dead than alive, lay trembling from head to foot in his hiding-place. At length the giant sat down quietly, while his wife served up his supper; and, on peeping through a crack in the oven-door, Jack was amazed at the quantities he devoured. When his meal was over, the giant called for his hen, which was accordingly brought and placed on the table; and every time he said, "Lay!" behold, the hen laid an egg of solid gold! Meanwhile his wife went to bed, and the giant, after amusing himself in this manner for a long while, grew drowsy

by degrees, and at length fell asleep at the table and snored like the roaring of a cannon. At daybreak, Jack, seeing him still asleep, crept out of his hiding-

39

place and ran off with the hen, and, finding his way to the bean-stalk, got down much better than he had expected. His mother was overjoyed at seeing him, for she had given him up as lost; nor was she less surprised when Jack told her he had brought home something which he hoped would make amends for his former follies, and produced the hen.

Both mother and son were now rich and happy, and lived for several months most comfortably, when Jack, recollecting the fairy's injunctions, determined to climb the bean-stalk again, to which his mother strongly objected, assuring him that the giant's wife would know better than to let him in, and that the giant would certainly kill him for stealing his hen. But Jack was so set upon going, that, after secretly procuring a disguise, and staining his skin with walnut-juice, he went forth one morning, and, climbing the bean-stalk, again made his way to the giant's house, which he reached towards evening, and again found the wife at the door. Jack made up a pitiful story to induce her to take him in for the night. The woman answered with the same objections as before, adding that she had taken in an ungrateful little vagabond, some months back, who had stolen one of her husband's treasures, ever since which he was fiercer than ever, and continually reproaching her. Jack, however, teased and teased till the good woman led him into the kitchen, and, after giving him a supper, hid him in a lumber-closet just as the giant walked in, and, after sniffing about, exclaimed, as before, "I smell fresh meat!" "Oh!" said the wife, "it is only the crows who have left a piece of raw meat on the roof of the house." So the giant grumbled a while, till his mouth was stopped by a supper fit for twenty aldermen, which his wife made haste to serve up; and, when he had eaten his fill, he desired to have his money-bags brought. Jack now peeped out of his hiding-place, and presently saw the wife return, dragging two heavy bags, one filled with new guineas, and the other with new shillings; and, on her complaining of the weight, the giant grew so exasperated that he would have struck her had she not hastily retreated. After counting up his treasure over and over again, the giant at length dropped off to sleep, and snored as loud as the rushing of the sea on a stormy night. Hereupon Jack put out first one foot and then another, and, approaching the table on tip-toe, seized the bags, and, slinging them over his shoulder, made his way to the bean-stalk, and, though almost bending beneath his burden, succeeded in climbing down safely. But

how grieved was he, on reaching the cottage-door, to find his mother so ill from over-anxiety on his account as to be almost dying! On seeing him safe,

42

however, she gradually recovered. Jack presented her the bags, their cottage was rebuilt and well furnished, and they lived very comfortably for about three years, during which the bean-stalk was not even mentioned by either of them.

But, at the end of that time, Jack, who had been thinking of it and looking at it stealthily for many a month past, felt so irresistibly impelled to try his luck once more, that one morning up he climbed, and, following the same road as on the two former occasions, he again found the giant's wife at the door,—only this time he had much more trouble to persuade her to let him in. Having succeeded at last, he was concealed in the copper by the time the giant returned with his usual alarming exclamation of "I smell fresh meat!" which Jack did not much mind at first, though he began to quail when the giant followed up his assertion by ferreting about in every corner of the kitchen, and even laying his little finger on the copper-lid, which sounded like the fall of a heavy beam. At length, supper drew off the giant's attention, and, when this was over, he told his wife to bring him his harp. When the instrument was placed on the table, the giant said, "Play!"

43

and it immediately struck up the most exquisite music imaginable, to which the giant, who was in a good humour, began to dance. Jack was so delighted that

he longed more for the harp than he had done for the other treasures ; and as the giant, not having much relish for sweet sounds, was quickly lulled to sleep,

41

he lifted the lid, got out of the copper, and seized the instrument. But the harp, being an enchanted one, called out, "Master! master!" which woke the giant, who started up and endeavoured to pursue Jack; but, having drunk a few tuns more than even his strong head could bear, he was only able to reel along, while Jack flew like the wind, and, clambering down the bean-stalk, called aloud for a hatchet, which was brought to him immediately; and just as the giant reached the top of the bean-stalk, Jack cut it close at the root, causing his foe to pitch headlong into the garden,—a fall that killed him on the spot.

Jack's mother was well pleased when she saw the bean-stalk cut down; and the fairy, having appeared, explained to her how she had bid her son undertake these journeys, and then, addressing Jack in turn, told him to be dutiful in future to his mother, and to follow his father's example by living to do good. She then vanished; but Jack never forgot her advice; and, begging his mother to forgive him all his past transgressions, he became a good son, and grew up to be a worthy man.

The Giant and the Brave Little Tailor.

ONE summer's morning, as a diminutive tailor was sitting on his table near the window, and plying his needle cheerfully, there came by a woman, crying, "Good jam, very cheap!" The tailor liked the notion of this: so he popped his little head out of window, and, calling to the woman, he told her, if she would come up, she would find a customer for her wares. The woman carried her heavy basket up three pair of stairs to the tailor, when he made her unpack all the pots, and, after examining and smelling them all, he said, "The jam seems good: so you may weigh me two ounces of it, my good woman: indeed, I don't mind if you make it a quarter of a pound."

The woman, who had expected a much larger purchase, served him as he desired, but went away grumbling. The tailor then went to a cupboard, and cut a slice of bread, and spread the jam upon it, and laid it beside him, as he thought he had better finish the doublet he was working at before he ate this dainty morsel. While he was stitching away as fast as he could, to get at it the sooner, the flies on the wall were attracted by the smell of the jam,

46

and down they came in flocks to partake of its sweets. "Nobody invited you," said the little tailor, as he brushed them away. Only, as the unbidden guests did not understand what he said, they were not to be put off, but returned in greater numbers than before, till the tailor was so exasperated that he snatched up a strip of cloth off his board, and flapped away till seven flies lay dead on the spot. "Am I such a desperado as all that comes to?" quoth he, as he counted the slain and admired his own bravery; "nay, then, the whole town shall hear of it." And the little tailor forthwith cut himself out a belt, on which he worked, in large letters, the words, "Seven at a blow." "The town, quotha!" continued he: "the whole world shall hear of it."

So he put on the belt, and sallied forth into the wide world, as his workshop was too narrow a stage for his bravery. Before he went, he looked about him to see what he could carry away with him, but he found nothing better than an old cheese, which he put into his pocket. After passing through the gates of the town, he perceived a bird that had got entangled in a bush, and this he caught and put into his pocket, in addition to the cheese; after which he pursued his way rapidly enough, for he was so light and nimble that he scarcely felt the least fatigue. The road he followed happened to lead to a mountain, and, on reaching its highest summit, he found a powerful giant sitting looking about him at the landscape around. The little tailor made up to him very boldly, saying, "Good-morning, comrade; and so you are looking at the wide world, are you? I am just going into it. Now, what say you to accompanying me?"

The giant looked at the tailor with the utmost contempt, and muttered, "You miserable wretch!" "Miserable wretch, indeed!" rejoined the little tailor, unbuttoning his coat and pointing to his belt: "only read and see what sort of a man I am." The giant read, "Seven at a blow," and, concluding it meant seven men the tailor had killed, began to entertain a greater degree of respect for the little fellow; but being, nevertheless, desirous of putting him to the proof, he picked up a stone, and squeezed it till the water dropped out of it. "Now do the same," said the giant, "if you have strength enough." "Is that all?" cried the little tailor: "that's a mere joke for me." And, putting his hand into his pocket, he drew out the cheese, and squeezed it till the whey oozed out.

48

"This is better still, I trow," observed he. The giant did not well know what to think or to say: so he picked up another stone, and threw it upwards to such a height that no eye could follow it. "There!" cried

he, "do as much if you can, my little fellow." "It's a good throw," returned the tailor, "but the stone must needs fall down again. Now, I'll throw something that sha'n't come back." And, drawing forth the bird from his pocket, he cast it into the air. De-

49

lighted at regaining its liberty, the bird, of course, never returned. "What say you to that?" asked the tailor. "It's a good throw," replied the giant; "but now let's see whether you are able to carry a tolerable weight." He then led the little tailor to a spot where lay a felled oak of considerable size, and bid him help him to carry it out of the forest, provided he had sufficient strength to do so. "Willingly," said the little man; "and if you do but place the trunk on your shoulder, I will lift up the branches, which are the heavier of the two." The giant accordingly shouldered the trunk of the tree, while the tailor sat down snugly on one of the branches, and, as his huge companion could not very well look round, he was tricked into carrying, not only the whole tree, but little Snip into the bargain. After they had gone a few steps, the giant could bear the weight no longer, and let fall the tree, while the tailor jumped nimbly down and pretended to be holding the branches, and laughed at the giant for being unable to carry a tree, though he was such a big fellow.

On going farther, they came to a cherry-tree, when the giant bent down the top, and, placing it in the tailor's hands, bid him eat of the fruit. Now, the tailor was much too weak to hold the branches, and, when the giant let them go, they whisked the tailor up into the air as they rebounded. "So," cried the giant, "it seems you have not strength to hold even such a switch as that?" "Oh," returned the tailor, "it is not the strength that fails me; but there is a sportsman shooting in yonder bush, and I had a mind to get out of his way. Jump after me if you can." The giant tried, but he could not manage to clear the tree, and remained hanging midway on one of the branches; so that the little tailor had the upper hand even this time.

"Since you are such a brave fellow," said the giant, "come and spend the night in our cavern." The little tailor made no bones to follow him, and they reached the cavern, where they found several other giants sitting by the fire, each eating a whole roast lamb for his supper. The giant then pointed to a bed, and told the tailor he might turn in and sleep there to his heart's content. But the bed was so large that the little man preferred creeping into a corner of the cavern. Towards midnight, when the giant thought he must be fast asleep, he took an iron club and shivered the bed at a single blow, making sure the little grasshopper that lay in it must be as dead as a door-nail. The next morning, when the giants sallied forth into the forest, and had forgotten all

about the little tailor, behold! he came up with them, looking as spruce and as bold as ever. The giants were frightened, and took to their heels as fast as they could.

52

As to our little Snip, he kept following his nose, and, after wandering a considerable way, he reached the courtyard of a royal palace, when, feeling tired, he stretched himself on the grass, and fell asleep. Some persons who happened to see him, and read "Seven at a blow" on his belt, immediately concluded he was a mighty warrior, and they hastened to inform the king of his arrival, observing, that it would be well to secure the services of such a man, in case war were to break out again. The king thought this advice was wise enough, and therefore sent one of his courtiers to be ready to offer the stranger to enter the army, as soon as he should awake. The courtier having delivered his message, the tailor said, "I came with the express intention of offering my services to his majesty." And he was accordingly received with all due honours, and placed in a residence by himself.

But the soldiers took umbrage at the little tailor's promotion, and wished him a thousand miles away, "For," said they, "suppose we should quarrel with him, he will kill seven of us at a blow, which is not to be borne." So they went to the king, and begged to be dismissed. Now, the king could not bear the idea of losing all his faithful adherents; yet he did not dare to send away the new-comer, lest he should kill both himself and his people, and take possession of the throne. So, after a good deal of reflection, he sent to the little tailor, to say that, as he was such a hero, he proposed to him to rid the land of a couple of giants who lived in a neighbouring forest, promising that, if he succeeded, he would give him his only daughter in marriage, and half his kingdom. He added that a hundred horse-soldiers should lend him their assistance. The little tailor thought it would be a fine thing to marry a beautiful princess: so he sent back word that he would soon tame the giants, and that he wanted no help, for he who could hit seven at a blow was not to be cowed by two.

The little tailor then sallied forth, followed by a hundred horse-soldiers; but, on reaching the forest, he told them to wait till he returned, as he meant to settle the giants' business alone. He then entered the thicket, and soon found the two giants snoring, under a tree. The little tailor lost no time in filling his pockets with stones, and then climbed up the tree, and, ensconcing himself in its branches, let fall several stones, one after another, right on the breast of one of the giants, who at length awoke, and, nudging

54

his companion, inquired why he beat him. "You
are dreaming," said the other: "I didn't touch you."
They then went to sleep again, when the tailor threw
down a stone that hit the other giant. "What are
you flinging stones at me for?" said the latter. "Nay,

man, you are dreaming," said the other. But, after
quarrelling a while, as they were both tired, they were
presently asleep again. The tailor then chose a very
thick stone, and hurled it with all his might at the
first giant. "This is too bad!" cried he, rising in a

fury and assailing his companion. The latter paid him in the same coin; and such was their mutual rage that they tore up whole trees, and never ceased belabouring each other till they both lay dead on the ground. The tailor now came down, and, drawing his sword, plunged it alternately into the breast of each of the slain giants, and then returned to the horse-soldiers, and told them he had overcome the giants. The soldiers however, would not believe him, till they had ridden into the forest, and seen the uprooted trees and the giants swimming in their blood.

The king, after he had got rid of his enemies, was not much pleased at the thought of giving up half his kingdom to the stranger: so he said, "You have not yet done. In the palace-court lies a bear, with whom you must pass the night, and if, when I rise in the morning, I find you still living, you shall have your reward." "Very well," said the tailor.

So, when evening came, our little tailor was led out and shut up in the court with the bear, who rose at once to give him a friendly welcome with his paw. "Softly, softly, my friend," said he: "I know a way to please you." Then, pulling out of his

56

pocket some fine walnuts, he cracked them, and ate the kernels. When the bear saw this, he longed for some too: so the tailor felt in his pocket and gave him a handful, not of walnuts, but nice round pebbles. The bear snapped them up, but could not

crack one of them, do what he would. Then said he to the tailor, "Friend, pray crack me the nuts." So the tailor took the stones, and slyly changed them for nuts, put them into his mouth, and crack! they went. "Oh!" said the bear, "now I see how you go to work, I am sure I can do it myself."

57

Then the tailor gave him the pebbles again, and the bear worked away as hard as he could, till he broke all his teeth, and lay down quite exhausted.

But the tailor began to think this would not last long: so he pulled a fiddle out from under his coat, and played him a tune. As soon as the bear heard it, he could not help jumping up and beginning to dance; and when he had jigged away for a while, he said, "Hark ye, friend! is the fiddle hard to play upon?" "No! not at all!" said the other. "Will you teach me to fiddle," said the bear, "so that I may have music whenever I want to dance?" "With all my heart; but let me look at your claws: they are so very long that I must first clip your nails a little bit." Then the bear lifted up his paws one after another, and the tailor tied them down tight, and said, "Now, wait till I come with my scissors." So he left the bear to growl as loud as he liked, and laid himself down on a heap of straw in the corner, and slept soundly. In the morning, when the king came, he found the tailor sitting comfortably at breakfast, and could no longer help keeping his word, but was obliged, willy-nilly, to give him his daughter and half his kingdom. So the wedding

58

was celebrated with much pomp, though with little joy, and the tailor became a king.

Some time after, the young queen heard her hus-

band talk in his sleep, and say, "Now, make haste, boy, and sew that waistcoat, and mend that coat, or I'll lay the yard-measure about your shoulders." She then guessed at the low origin of her spouse, and the next day she went and begged her father to get her rid of a husband who was nothing better than a tailor. The king bid her be of good cheer, and promised, if she left her chamber-door open on the following night, he would send his servants to bind him in his sleep, and take him on board a ship, which should carry him away forever. But it happened their conversation was overheard by one of the king's squires, who liked the young stranger, and went and told him of the danger that threatened him. So, when the tailor had gone to bed, he pretended to fall asleep, and, as soon as his wife had opened the door, he spoke as if he were talking in his sleep, and said, "Make haste, boy, and sew that waistcoat, and mend that coat, or I'll lay the yard-measure about your shoulders. I have hit seven at a stroke, killed two giants, and tamed a bear: so I need not fear those who stand without." On hearing this, the folk outside were so frightened that they ran away like chaff before the wind, and no one ever dared to lay a finger on him. So a king he was, and a king little Snip remained all the days of his life.

Little Maia.

THERE once lived a woman who so regretted not having any children that she at last applied to an old witch, telling her she would be reduced to beg, borrow, or even steal an infant, unless she could assist her to find one. "There is no need to do that," said the witch: "only take this barleycorn, which is of quite a different kind to what ploughmen sow in the fields, and plant it in a flower-pot, and you will see what a rare blossom it will bring you."

The woman thanked her and gave her twelve shillings; and the moment she reached home she planted the barleycorn, that soon grew up into a beautiful large flower, that seemed to promise to be something like a tulip, as far as could be judged from the bud. The woman was delighted at the sight of it, but her raptures were unbounded when the leaves unfolded and discovered a most exquisite and delicately-formed little girl, not above an inch high, to whom she gave the name of Maia.

A neatly-varnished walnut-shell made a cradle for the diminutive creature, her mattress was of violets, and a rose-leaf served as her counterpane. During the daytime she played on the table, where her foster-mother had placed a plate, encircled by a wreath of flowers, with their stems in the water. A large tulip-leaf served as a boat, in which Maia rowed about on this miniature lake with a couple of oars, each consisting of a single white horse-hair. She would sing, too, with a tiny voice of the most delicious quality.

One night, as she lay in her pretty bed, a nasty, ugly wet toad jumped into the room through a broken pane in the window, and alighted on the table, while she slept beneath her rosy counterpane. "She would make a charming wife for my son," thought the toad; and, taking up the walnut-shell, Maia, and all, she hopped back into the garden. It was here she lived, on the bank of a broad stream, together with her son, who was as frightful as herself, and said nothing but "Croak! croak!" when he saw the beautiful little creature.

"Not so loud," quoth the mother toad, "or you will wake her, and she might escape from us. We will lay her on the acanthus-leaves in the middle of the stream, which will serve as an island for so small and light a being, and then she will not be

62

able to run away while we prepare the state apart-
ment under the swamp."

Accordingly, the old toad placed her on the
broadest acanthus-leaf that spread its green surface
on the water.

When the little creature woke in the morning and
found herself surrounded by water, she began to cry
bitterly; but her fright was increased when the toad,
after decking her chamber with reeds and flowers
for the reception of her intended daughter-in-law,
swam up to the acanthus-leaf in company with her
son, and presented him to Maia, saying, "This is
your future husband; and you shall presently see
what an elegant residence has been prepared for you

63

in the swamp." "Croak! croak!" was all the son could say in confirmation of his mother's assertion.

They then swam away with the pretty cradle to place it in the bride's future abode, while Maia remained alone on the acanthus, and wept at the very thought of marrying a hideous toad. The little fishes, who had heard all that had passed, now popped their heads out of the water to see the tiny maiden, and, when they found how pretty she was, they declared it would be a shame to let her be sacrificed to a loathsome toad; and accordingly they all assembled round the stem of the leaf she sat upon, and nibbled and nibbled till they set it free, and it floated down the stream, carrying little Maia far beyond the reach of her uncouth bridegroom.

Away she sailed past a number of cities, till she was fairly out of the land, and reached a beautiful country where the sun was shining like gold upon the water. Here she was seen by a cockchafer, who pounced down on the fragile equipage, and, encircling her in his claws, bore her off to a tree. Oh, how frightened was poor little Maia! But she soon saw the cockchafer meant no harm, for he placed her on the greenest leaf that grew upon the tree,

64

and gave her some honey from its blossoms to eat, and told her she was a sweet little creature, though so unlike a cockchafer. Presently, some female cockchafers, who lived in the same tree, came to see her, but they turned up their feelers very disdainfully as they observed that the pitiful thing had only two legs! and they all, with one voice, declared her to be extremely ugly.

The cockchafer, seeing that his female friends held her so cheap, finished by thinking that he was mistaken about her beauty, and declared he no longer cared about her, and that she might go away wherever she liked. They then flew down with little Maia, and placed her on a daisy, where she sat and wept to think that she was so ugly that even the cockchafers would not let her remain among them.

Poor little Maia lived all alone in the forest the whole summer through. She made herself a hammock of plaited grass-blades, which she hung under a burdock-leaf, to be safe from showers: the honey drawn from flowers served for her food, and dewdrops for her drink; and all this was vastly pleasant so long as summer, or even autumn, lasted. But when winter came, and the birds had ceased to sing, and the trees and flowers had withered, and the large burdock-leaf that served for her shelter was completely shrivelled up, leaving nothing but a bare stem, then it was quite a different story, and poor little Maia was nearly frozen to death; especially when the snow began to fall, for every flake was to her like what a shovelful would be to ordinary human beings. So she sallied forth from the wood into

a corn-field that lay close by, where there was nothing but the dry, hard stubble left, which, proportionately to her, seemed an immense forest. After

66

wandering a long while, she reached a narrow opening that led to the dwelling of a field-mouse, who had burrowed a safe retreat under the stubble, where she lived very snugly, and had a chamber full of corn, and an excellent kitchen and dining-room. Poor Maia just ventured into the passage, like a beggar, and requested a little bit of a barleycorn, as she had not tasted food for nearly a couple of days.

"Why, you diminutive creature!" cried the field-mouse, who was a good-hearted old body in the main, "come into my warm room and dine with me."

And Maia pleased her so well that she told her she might stay with her all the winter, provided she would keep the rooms clean and tidy and tell her amusing stories. Maia did as the old field-mouse required of her, and they lived very comfortably together.

"We shall soon have a visit from a neighbour of mine, who comes to see me once a week," said the field-mouse. "He is much better off than I am, and has a fine large house, and wears a beautiful black velvet tippet. You would be a lucky girl, indeed, if you got him for a husband! So, as he can't see at all, you must mind and tell him all your best stories, to try and please him."

67

But Maia had no notion of marrying a mole; and, when he came in his fine black velvet tippet, to visit his neighbour, she made little account either of his boasted learning or of his fine house, which the field-mouse frequently said was at least twenty times larger than her own; for he professed to dislike both

flowers and sunshine, and that simply because he had never seen them! However, Maia was obliged to sing; and her voice was so sweet that the mole fell at once in love with her, though, being a prudent character, he said nothing of the kind till he had taken time for reflection.

As the mole had lately burrowed a long passage leading from his house to his neighbour's, he gave the field-mouse and Maia leave to walk there whenever they liked, but warned them not to be afraid of the dead bird that was lying on the ground, and which he had found by accident on turning up the earth as he hollowed out the passage. The mole then showed them the way through the long dark winding, and when they came near the spot where lay the bird, he bored a hole through the roof with his broad nose, so as to let in light, and they perceived a dead swallow, with its beautiful wings closely pressed to its sides and its feet and head drawn up under its feathers. It was evident he had been frozen to death. Maia felt pained for the poor little thing, for she was very fond of birds; but the unfeeling mole only pushed him out of the way, observing, "He will not pipe any more. Thank God I was not born a bird, who can say nothing but 'twit! twit!' and is obliged to die of hunger when winter sets in!"

"That is a sensible remark of yours, neighbour," quoth dame field-mouse.

But, when these two worthies had turned their backs, little Maia returned and kissed the bird's closed eyes. "For who knows," said she, "but it may be one of those who sang to me so sweetly during the summer?"

The mole now stopped up the hole again, and the ladies returned home. But Maia could not sleep that night; so she got out of bed and plaited a hay coverlet, which she took and spread over the dead swallow, and then laid some soft wool, which she had found in her mistress's chamber, on each side of the bird, to keep him warm as he lay on the cold earth. When she had concluded her pious offices, just as she bent down to give the bird a parting kiss, she was half frightened at feeling something within his breast; for he was not dead, but only benumbed by cold, and the warm covering had brought him back to life. Maia trembled with fear, because the bird was so large, compared to herself; yet she took courage, and ran to fetch a mint-leaf, which served her for a counterpane, and laid it over his head.

On the following night she went to see him, but, though alive, she found him so weak that he could only thank her in a faint voice and express a wish to get back into the sunshine, to be restored to strength. But Maia told him that the snow lay on the ground, and that he must remain for a while in his warm bed, and she would take care of him. She then brought him a draught of water in a leaf, and he told her how his wing had been torn by a bramble, which prevented his joining his fellow-swallows

in their flight, and how he had fallen exhausted on the ground, and been so benumbed by the cold that he knew not what became of him afterwards.

So the swallow spent the winter under ground, and was kindly waited on by Maia, unknown to either the field-mouse or the mole, both of whom hated birds; and when spring came again, she opened the hole for the bird to depart. As he was about to sally forth into the sunny atmosphere, the swallow told Maia that, if she would come with him, he could easily carry her on his back. But Maia refused, for she knew the old field-mouse would be sorry to part with her. "Then farewell, thou sweet, kind girl!" cried the swallow, as he flew away; and poor Maia watched him with tearful eyes.

The corn which had been sown about the field-mouse's dwelling had now sprung up and formed rows of lofty trees, according to Maia's estimate, and she would fain have rambled beneath their shade, but dame field-mouse would not let her go a-gadding. "You must make your wedding-outfit during the summer," said the thrifty mouse, "against you become the mole's wife;" for that tiresome personage had asked her in marriage of the field-mouse. So Maia was set to spin, and four spiders were employed day and night to forward the preparations; and the mole came to court her every evening. But Maia could not abide the stupid creature; and when she stole up every morning and evening to peep at the blue sky between the ears of corn, she wished the swallow back again, though she had little hope of his ever returning.

When autumn came, her wedding-clothes were all ready, and the field-mouse told her that in another month the marriage should take place; but Maia wept, and said she would not marry the nasty mole. "Nonsense!" cried the mouse; "don't talk such stuff, or I shall bite you. You ought to be thankful for such a husband."

Then Maia was very sad to think she would have to live under ground, and never see the earth's fair face, even as much as she had done at the field-mouse's, and she went to take a last leave of the sun. The harvest was now over, and, as she leant upon a little red flower that still remained, and looked mournfully up at the sky, she heard "Twit! twit!" above her head, and in another moment her friend the swallow was by her side. She then related her troubles to him, when he told her to mount upon his back and fasten herself securely with her girdle, and he would bear her far beyond the mole's reach, to a beautiful warm land where the summer was perpetual. This time Maia willingly consented, and away the swallow flew with her over the woods and

the sea beyond, and across the snow-capped mountains, till they reached a lovely climate, where
grapes and citrons were growing and butterflies
disporting. But the swallow did not stop here, but
flew to a more distant and delicious country, where,

on the shores of the blue ocean, stood the ruins of
a white marble palace, at the top of whose vine-
wreathed columns a number of his fellow-birds had
built their nests. "This is my home," said the
swallow; "but I will set you down among those

74

pretty white flowers that grow between the broken fragments of yon fallen pillar." So saying, he placed her on one of the broad leaves, when she was surprised to see a little manikin, as white and transparent as glass, with wings on his shoulders and a gold crown on his head, standing in the midst of the flower. Every flower contains a male or a female spirit of the same kind, but this was the king of them all. "Oh, how handsome he is!" cried Maia to the swallow. And when the prince had recovered from his fright at the giant bird, he was in turn so delighted at Maia's beauty that he took off his crown and placed it on her brow, and asked her to become his wife and the queen over all the flowers. This was rather a different match from the toad or the mole! So little Maia soon said, "Yes," and there stepped forth from each flower a little lady or a manikin, who brought her presents,—the best among which was a pair of wings about the size of those of a large fly, which they fastened to her shoulders, and which enabled her to fly from flower to flower; and then great rejoicings were held, and the swallow sang his sweetest songs to the newly-wedded pair, and brought back the story of little Maia.

The Eleven Wild Swans.

In the land whither the swallows fly to seek a home in winter, there once lived a king who had eleven sons, and one daughter, named Elisa. The eleven young

princes used to go to school, and write on golden slates with diamond pencils; while their sister Elisa sat upon a crystal stool, and had a book, full of pretty pictures, that was worth half a kingdom. Oh, what happy children they were! But, unfortunately, they were not destined to continue so much longer; for their father married again, and the new queen was very unkind to them. And this they perceived in the very first few days, when the palace was full of company, and there was plenty of feasting; for, instead of the cakes and apples that used to fall to their share on such occasions, their step-mother gave them some sand, and told them they might play at eating and drinking.

On the following week, the queen sent little Elisa away into the country, to be brought up in a cottage by a homely couple, and she spoke so ill of the poor princes to their father, that he ceased to care any thing about them. The wicked creature then said to them, "Fly away into the wide world; you shall become large birds without any voices." But she could not completely accomplish her malicious intentions, and the young princes were changed into eleven beautiful wild swans, who immediately flew out of the palace-windows, with a peculiar cry, far over the garden and the wood beyond.

It was early in the morning as they passed by the cottage where their sister lay asleep. Here they hovered over the roof and flapped their wings, but all to no purpose, as nobody saw or heard them: so they took their flight onward, till they reached a thick forest that stretched away to the sea-shore.

Poor little Elisa meantime remained secluded in the peasant's cottage till she was fifteen, when the queen was obliged to fetch her home; but, when she saw how pretty she was grown, she hated her in her heart, and would gladly have changed her likewise into a swan, had not the king insisted on seeing his daughter. Not daring to do this, she stained her skin with walnut-juice, rubbed her lovely face with rancid ointment, and tousled her hair, so that it was impossible to recognize her, and when her father saw her he was quite shocked, and exclaimed that she was not his daughter. Poor Elisa then wept bitterly, and slunk out of the palace, and wandered till she reached a large forest.

She had not been long in the forest before night came on, and she lay down on the moss and went to sleep, and dreamed of her brothers. When she awoke, the sun was already high in the heavens, the birds were singing blithely, and a number of rivulets ran babbling along till they all fell into a small lake, so transparent that every leaf could be seen reflected on its pure surface. When our little wanderer looked into this natural mirror, she was frightened to see how brown and ugly she had become; but no sooner had she washed her face in its waters than her skin resumed all its whiteness.

On pursuing her journey, she met an old woman, of whom she inquired whether she had seen eleven princes riding through the forest.

"No," replied the old woman; "but yesterday I saw eleven wild swans, with gold crowns on their heads, swimming near the banks of the stream close by here."

79

She then led Elisa to the brow of a hill, at the foot of which ran a stream overshaded by trees, whose drooping branches hung into the water. Elisa took leave of her aged companion, and walked along till the stream flowed towards a wide, open shore. The ocean now lay before the young princess; but not a sail was to be seen, nor was a human voice to be heard; only among the sea-weeds she perceived eleven swan's feathers, which gave her hopes she should find her brothers at last. Sure enough, just at sunset Elisa perceived eleven wild swans, with gold crowns on their heads, flying towards the land, one behind another, like a long white ribbon. They alighted on the hill; and no sooner had the sun sunk to rest in the ocean, than their swans' skins fell off, and they appeared as so many young men. The princess shrieked with joy, for she recognized her brothers, notwithstanding they had now grown to manhood's estate, and she ran to embrace them, calling them by their names. The brothers were no less delighted to see their sister, and they had soon mutually related how ill their step-mother had behaved to them. The eldest brother then said, "We fly about as wild swans so long as the sun remains on the horizon, but we recover our human shape the instant it has set. We are, therefore, always obliged to look out for a resting-place towards sunset, for, should night surprise us up in the clouds, we would fall down into the sea on becoming human beings. We live in a lovely land beyond the sea; but it is a long way thither, and we have to cross the ocean, where the only footing we can find for the night is on a little rock just large enough to allow us to sit side by side, and where the waves wash over us in rough weather. Yet we perform this troublesome voyage once a year, for the sake of visiting our native land. Here we are allowed to remain but eleven days, during which we fly over the forest, so as to behold the palace where our father dwells, and where we spent our happy childhood in our mother's lifetime. We have now only two days left to tarry in these climes; but what shall we do to take you with us, dear little sister, when we have neither ship nor boat?"

They continued talking together nearly half the night, until the princess fell asleep from sheer fatigue. She was awakened in the morning by the rustling of her brothers' wings overhead, as they flew away, all except the youngest, who came and nestled in Elisa's lap. She stroked his wings and caressed him, and

81

they remained together the whole day. Towards evening the others returned, and, when they had recovered their natural form, they told their sister they would be obliged to fly away on the morrow, but

that, if she were not afraid, they felt their wings were strong enough to carry her across the sea. "Yes; do take me," cried Elisa; and they spent the greater part

82

of the night in making a net with rushes and the
pliant bark of willows, which was strong enough to
bear the princess ; and when she had lain down upon
it and fallen asleep, her brothers, on becoming swans
at sunrise, lifted it with their beaks and flew up to the
clouds, while one of them spread his wings over her to
shade her face from the sun.   Elisa did not wake till
they were far out at sea, and it seemed like a dream
when she found herself borne so high in the air that
the ships below looked no larger than sea-gulls; and
fearful, indeed, it was, to be flying betwixt air and
water for the livelong day !   Nor could the swans fly
so fast as when unclogged by their precious burden.
And this Elisa felt, and, when the sun was fast dis-
appearing, and no rock appeared in sight, her heart
misgave her, and she reproached herself bitterly for
having exposed them to the danger of resuming their
shape too soon and falling into the sea and getting
drowned for her sake.   But, lo and behold, when the
sun was nearly hid in the waves, she perceived a rock
that looked no bigger than a sea-dog's head, peeping
above the waves, and, just as the parting rays of daylight seemed to go out suddenly, like the sparks of a
piece of burnt paper, they alighted safe and sound on

their narrow footing, where there was barely room
for one more than their usual number.

At the dawn of day, the swans flew onward with
their sister, and before the sun had sunk to rest they

had reached the shores of a beautiful land. She then
went to sleep in a pretty grotto hung with elegant
creeping plants that looked like richly-embroidered
tapestry; and, as her waking and sleeping thoughts
were always running on the same subject, namely, how
her brothers were to be delivered from the spell that

bound them, it was no wonder that she dreamed she was flying up in the air to Fata Morgana's castle, which she had seen as they came along, and that the fairy, who, though young and beautiful, still bore a

distant resemblance to the old woman who had told her where to find the swans, said to her, " The spell may be broken, but it requires great courage and per-severance to attempt it. You see this nettle that I hold in my hand? A number of the same sort grow around the cave in which you are sleeping; but those only, and such as grow on graves in churchyards, are available for the purpose required. You must pluck them, though they will blister your hands, and by treading them with your feet you will obtain flax, with which you must plait eleven coats of mail with long sleeves, and by putting these on the eleven swans the enchantment will be broken. But, remember, from the moment you begin your work until it is concluded, though it should last a year, you must not utter a syllable, or the first word you speak would pierce your brothers' hearts like a dagger."

So saying, the fairy touched Elisa's hand with the nettle, which stung her so sharply that she immediately awoke, and by her side she saw a nettle exactly similar to the one in her dream. She at once went out and gathered a number of nettles. They blistered her hands most dreadfully; but she heeded not the pain, and only thought of saving her brothers. After treading out the nettles with her bare feet, she began to plait a coat of mail with the green flax thus obtained. When the brothers came back in the evening, they were frightened at finding their sister dumb; but on looking at her hands they guessed what she was enduring for their

sakes, and the youngest brother wept from mingled
pity and gratitude, and where his tears fell the blis-
ters disappeared. She continued working all night,
and during the following day, while the swans were
absent. One coat of mail was now finished, and she
began a second. As she was busy gathering more
nettles, she heard the sound of a hunting-horn, and
flew back in alarm to her grotto, where she was presently followed by a pack of hounds and huntsmen,
the handsomest among whom was the king of the
land. "Where do you come from, my beautiful
maid?" said the king, who had never beheld any face
so lovely before. Elisa only shook her head, for she
dared not speak. "Come with me," said the king,
"and you shall be dressed in silk and velvet, and wear
a gold crown, and live in my palace." So saying,
he lifted her on to his horse and carried her away,
though she wept and wrung her hands. At sunset
they reached the royal residence, and she was taken
through a splendid suite of rooms, to a chamber where
a number of ladies' maids dressed her in the most
sumptuous clothes, and drew gloves over her poor
sore fingers ; and when she appeared again amidst
the courtiers, she looked so beautiful that they all

bowed down to her, and the king chose her for his bride,—though the archbishop muttered something about witchcraft, and did not half like the notion of such a marriage. But the king did not attend to him, and ordered the music to strike up, while a costly supper was brought in, and the loveliest girls began to dance round the princess. But nothing could win a smile from her. Then the king led her to a little cabinet next to her sleeping-chamber, which was carpeted with a rich green carpet, and where lay the bundle of flax which she had made out of the nettles, and the coat of mail, which one of the huntsmen had brought away as a curiosity, and said to her, "You can here fancy yourself in your early home, and compare your former rough work with your present queenly state." When Elisa heard this, she looked pleased for the first time, and kissed the king's hand, and he was so delighted that he caused all the bells in the kingdom to be rung, and he raised the dumb girl to the throne. The new queen loved the king for his kindness, and was sorry she could not tell him what lay so heavy on her heart, and she often got up at night and slipped away to advance her work; but when she began the seventh coat of mail she was short of flax. She, therefore, went out one night to the churchyard to gather more nettles, and passed by a set of hideous witches, who feed on corpses, when she happened to be seen by the archbishop, who informed the king next day of what he had witnessed. The king, though loath to believe any thing against his wife, watched her closely the following night, while pretending to be asleep, and saw her get up and disappear. The same occurrence took place night after night, till she had completed all but one coat of mail, when, requiring some more flax, she stole out to the churchyard, followed by the king and the archbishop. When the king saw her pass by the horrid witches, he believed her guilty, and said, with a sigh, "The people must judge her;" and the people condemned her to be burnt as a witch. She was then thrown into a dungeon, with nothing to lie upon but the nettles and the rough coats of mail; but this was a source of joy to her, as it enabled her to continue her work. Towards evening her youngest brother came and flapped his wings against her prison-bars, as if to bid her take heart; and before sunrise the eleven princes repaired to the palace, and requested an audience of the king; but he was asleep, and nobody dared to disturb him, and by dawn of day they were fain to fly over the roof as so many swans. The poor queen was now led forth, in sackcloth, on a miserable cart, still working at the eleventh coat of mail, while the ten others lay around her. The populace taunted her, and would have torn her work to pieces, when eleven swans flew down, and, settling on the cart, kept flapping their wings. The mob then cried, "A miracle! she is innocent!" and, just as the executioner was about to seize her, she hastily slipped the eleven coats over the swans, who instantly became eleven handsome princes,—only the youngest had a wing instead of an arm, as she had not had time to finish the sleeve. "Yes, I am innocent!" cried she, "for now I may speak." And the populace knelt before her as to a saint, while she fainted away from exhaustion. · The eldest brother then related all that had happened, and while he spoke every fagot on the pile had taken root, and became a beautiful rose, and at the top of all bloomed a white rose, which the king gathered, and laid on Elisa's bosom, when she returned to life and happiness. And then the bells pealed merrily, and a feast was held, the like of which had never been seen before.

90

Bold Robin Hood.

THE famous ROBIN HOOD was born at Locksley, Nottinghamshire, about 1160. He was a handsome youth, and the best archer in the county, and regularly bore away the prizes at all the archery-meetings, being able to strike a deer five hundred yards off. In truth, he was just fit to be one of the royal archers, and would, no doubt, have turned out better, had not his uncle been persuaded by the monks of Fountain Abbey to leave all his property to the Church; and thus poor Robin, being sent adrift into the world, took refuge in Sherwood Forest, where he met with several other youths, who soon formed themselves into a band under his leadership and commenced leading the life of outlaws. Robin Hood and his men adopted a uniform of Lincoln green, with a scarlet cap; and each man was armed with a dagger and a basket-hilted sword, and a bow in his hand, and a quiver slung on his back, while the captain always had a bugle-horn with him to summon his followers about him.

One day, when Robin Hood set out alone in hopes of meeting with some adventure, he reached a brook, over which a narrow plank was laid to serve for a bridge, and, just as he was going to cross it, a tall

and handsome stranger appeared on the other side,
and, as neither seemed disposed to give way, they
met in the middle of the bridge.

"Go back," cried the stranger to Robin Hood,
"or it will be the worse for you."

But Robin Hood laughed at the idea of his giving
way to anybody, and proposed they should each take
an oak branch and fight it out. Accordingly, they
set to in right earnest; and, after thrashing each

92

other well, the stranger gave Robin Hood a blow on his head, which effectually pitched him into the water. When Robin Hood had waded back to the bank, he put his bugle to his lips, and blew several blasts, till the forest rang again, and his followers came leaping from all directions to see what their captain wanted. When he had told them how he had been served by the stranger, they would fain have ducked him; but Robin Hood, who admired his bravery, proposed to him to join their band.

"Here's my hand on it," cried the stranger, delighted at the proposal. "Though my name is John Little, you shall find I can do great things."

But Will Stutely, one of Robin's merry men, insisted upon it that he must be re-christened: so a feast was held, a barrel of ale broached, and the new-comer's name was changed from John Little to Little John, which nickname, seeing that he was near seven feet high, was a perpetual subject for laughter.

Not long after this, as Robin Hood sat one morning by the wayside trimming his bow and arrows, there rode by a butcher with a basket of meat, who was hastening to market. After bidding him good-morrow, Robin asked what he would take for the

93

horse and the basket. The butcher, somewhat surprised, answered he would not care to sell them for
less than four silver marks. "Do but throw your
greasy frock into the bargain," said Robin, "and
here's the money." Glad of so good a bargain, the
butcher lost no time in dismounting and throwing off
his smock-frock, which the outlaw put on over his
clothes, and then galloped away to Nottingham.

On reaching the town, Robin Hood put up his horse
at an inn, and then went into the market, and, un-
covering his basket, began to sell its contents about
five times cheaper than all the other butchers. The
other butchers could not at first understand why
everybody flocked to purchase his goods in preference to theirs; but when they heard that he had
sold a leg of pork for a shilling, they consulted together, and agreed that he must be some rich man's
son, who was after a frolic, or else a downright mad-
man, and that they had better try and learn something
more about him, or else he would ruin their business.
So, when the market was over, one of them invited
Robin Hood to dine with their company. The Sheriff
of Nottingham presided at the head of the table,
while at the other end sat the innkeeper. The out-

law played his part as well as the rest of them; and
when the dishes were removed, he called for more
wine, telling them all to drink as much as they could
carry, and he would pay the reckoning.

The sheriff then turned to Robin Hood, and asked
him whether he had any horned beasts to sell. Robin
Hood replied he had some two or three hundreds;

95

whereupon the sheriff said that, as he wanted a few heads of cattle, he would like to ride over and look at them that same day. So Robin flung down a handful of silver on the table, by way of farewell to his astonished companions, and set out for Sherwood Forest with the sheriff, who had mounted his palfrey, and provided himself with a bag of gold for his purchase. The outlaw was so full of jokes and merriment as they went along that the sheriff thought he had never fallen in with a pleasanter fellow. On a sudden, however, the sheriff recollected that the woods were infested by Robin Hood and his band, and he said to his companion he hoped they would not meet with any of them, to which he only answered by a loud laugh. Presently they reached the forest, when a herd of deers crossed their path. "How do you like my horned beasts, Master Sheriff?" inquired Robin. "To tell you the truth," replied the sheriff, "I only half like your company, and wish myself away from hence." Then Robin Hood put his bugle to his mouth and blew three blasts, when about a hundred men, with Little John at their head, immediately surrounded them, and the latter inquired what his master wanted. "I have brought the Sheriff of Notting-

ham to dine with us," said Rooin. "He is welcome,"
quoth Little John; "and I hope he will pay well for
his dinner." They then took the bag of gold from
the luckless sheriff, and counted out three hundred
pounds; after which Robin asked him if he would
like some venison for dinner. But the sheriff told
him to let him go, or he would rue the day: so the
outlaw desired his best compliments to his good
dame, and wished him a pleasant journey home.

But, if Robin loved a joke, he often did a good turn
to those who needed his assistance. Thus, he lent four
hundred golden pounds to Sir Rychard o' the Lee, who
had mortgaged his lands of Wierysdale for that sum to
St. Mary's Abbey, and who happened to pass through
Sherwood Forest on his way to York, to beg the abbot
to grant him another year. Robin Hood, moreover,
bid Little John accompany him as his squire. When
they reached the city, the superior was seated in his
hall, and declared to the brethren that if Sir Rychard
did not appear before sunset his lands would be for-
feited. Presently the Knight of Wierysdale came in,
and pretended to beg for mercy; but the proud abbot
spurned him, when Sir Rychard flung the gold at his
feet and snatched away the deed, telling him if he had

shown a little Christian mercy he should not only have
returned the money, but made a present to the abbey.

Another time, as Robin Hood was roaming through
the forest, he saw a handsome young man coming

along with disordered clothes and dishevelled hair,
and sighing deeply at every step. Robin Hood, having sent one of his men to fetch him, inquired what

lay so heavy on his heart. The young man pulled out his purse, and showed him a ring, saying, "I bought this yesterday to marry a maiden I have courted these seven long years, and this morning she is gone to church to wed another." "Does she love you?" said Robin. "She has told me so a hundred times," answered Allen-a-Dale, for such was the youth's name. "Tut, man! then she is not worth caring for, if she be so fickle!" cried Robin. "But she does not love him," interrupted Allen-a-Dale; "he is an old cripple, quite unfit for such a lovely lass." "Then why does she marry him?" inquired Robin. "Because the old knight is rich, and her parents insist upon it, and have scolded and raved at her till she is as meek as a lamb." "And where is the wedding to take place?" said Robin. "At our parish, five miles from hence," said Allen; "and the Bishop of Hereford, the bridegroom's brother, is to perform the ceremony."

Then, without more ado, Robin Hood dressed himself up as a harper, with a flowing white beard and a dark-coloured mantle, and, bidding twenty-four of his men follow at a distance, he entered the church and took his place near the altar. Presently the old knight appeared, hobbling along, and handing in a maiden as fair as day, all tears and blushes, accompanied by her young companions strewing flowers. "This is not a fit match," said Robin, aloud; "and I forbid the marriage." And then, to the astonishment of the bishop and of all present, he blew a blast on his horn, when four-and-twenty archers came leaping into the churchyard and entered the building. Foremost among these was Allen-a-Dale, who presented his bow to Robin Hood. The outlaw by this time had cast off his cloak and false beard, and, turning to the bride, said, "Now, pretty one, tell me freely whom you prefer for a husband,—this gouty old knight, or one of these bold young fellows?" "Alas!" said the young maid, casting down her eyes, "Allen-a-Dale has courted me for seven long years; and he is the man I would choose." "Then now, my good lord bishop," said Robin, "prithee unite this loving pair before we leave the church." "That cannot be," said the bishop: "the law requires they should be asked three times in the church." "If that is all," quoth Robin, "we'll soon settle that matter." Then, pulling off the bishop's gown, he dressed Little John up in it, gave him the book, and bid him ask them seven times in the church, lest three should not be enough. Robin

100

Hood gave away the maiden; and the whole company had a venison dinner in Sherwood Forest; and from that day Allen-a-Dale was a staunch friend to Robin Hood as long as he lived.

Robin Hood had often heard tell of the prowess of a certain Friar Tuck, who, having been expelled from Fountain's Abbey for his irregular conduct, lived in a rude hut he had built himself amidst the woods, and who was said to wield a quarter-staff and let fly an arrow better than any man in Christendom. So, being anxious to see how far this was true, Robin set off one morning for Fountain's Dale, where he found the friar rambling on the bank of the river Skell. The outlaw walked up to him, saying, "Carry me over this water, thou brawny friar, or thou hast not an hour to live." The friar tucked up his gown, and carried him over without a word; but when Robin seemed to be going, he cried out, "Stop, my fine fellow, and carry me over this water, or it shall breed you pain." Robin did so, and then said, "As you are double my weight, it is fair I should have two rides to your one : so carry me back again." The friar again took Robin on his back; but, on reaching the middle of the stream, he pitched him into the water, saying, "Now,

my fine fellow, let's see whether you'll sink or swim."
Robin swam to the bank, and said, "I see you are
worthy to be my match;" and then, summoning his
foresters by a blast of his bugle he told the friar he

was Robin Hood, and asked him to join his band.
"If there's an archer among you that can beat me
at the long-bow, then I'll be your man," quoth Friar
Tuck. Then, pointing to a hawk on the wing, he
added, "I'll kill it, and he who can strike it again

102

before it falls will be the better man of the two." Little John accepted the challenge. The shafts flew off; and when the dead bird was picked up, it was found that the friar's arrow had pinioned the hawk's wings to his sides, and that Little John's had trans- fixed it from breast to back. So Friar Tuck owned himself outdone, and joined Robin's merry men.

One morning six priests passed through Sherwood Forest, on richly-caparisoned horses; and, thinking a good prize was in the wind, the outlaws bid them halt, and Friar Tuck seized the bridle of the one whom he judged to be the abbot, and bid him pay the toll. The abbot got down, and gave him a cuff that made his ears tingle; then Robin flung him on his knees, and plucked him by the beard. Quoth Friar Tuck, "We don't take that sort of coin." "But we are going on a message from King Richard," said the abbot. Then Robin bid the friar desist, say- ing, "God save the king, and confound all his foes!" "You are a noble fellow," quoth the abbot; "and if you and your men will give up this lawless life and become my archers, you shall have the king's par- don." He then opened his gown, and Robin Hood and his archers, guessing at once that Richard him-

103

self stood before them, bent their knees to their liege lord, crying, "Long live King Richard!"

So Robin Hood accompanied the king to London, followed by fifty of his most faithful adherents; and here he assumed the title of Earl of Huntingdon. But he soon grew tired of the confinement of court,

104

and asked permission to revisit the woods. The king granted him seven days; but, when once he breathed the pure air of Sherwood again, he could not tear himself away; and when, from old habit, he sounded his bugle, he was surprised to see the signal answered by fourscore youths. Little John soon joined him, and he again became the leader of a band. King Richard was so enraged on hearing this, that he sent two hundred soldiers to reduce the rebel; and a desperate fight took place on a plain in the forest, when Robin Hood was wounded by an arrow, and removed to Kirkley's Nunnery, where the treacherous prioress suffered him to bleed to death. Seeing his end fast approaching, he called to Little John, and begged him to remove him to the woods, and there poor Robin Hood died, as he had lived, beneath the green trees, and was buried according to his wish. The stone that marked the spot bore the following inscription:—

> " Here, underneath this little stone,
> Lies Robert, Earl of Huntingdon.
> Ne'er archer was as he so good;
> And people call'd him 'Robin Hood.'
> Such outlaws as he and his men
> Will England never see again."

The Nine Mountains.

THERE once lived in the village of Rambin an honest hard-working peasant, named Jacob Dietrich, who supported his wife and family on the labor of his hands. Of all their children, none, perhaps, was so dear to the parents as Johnny, the youngest, who was the prettiest and liveliest little fellow ever seen, and was always perfect in his tasks at school, and well-behaved at home. When Johnny was eight years old, he spent the summer at his uncle's, who was a farmer in Rodenkirchen; and here he used to be sent, together with the other boys, to drive the cows into the meadows near the nine mountains, where they sat and watched them all day long. It happened that an old cowherd, called Klas Stark-wolt, used to bring his cattle the same way, and frequently joined the boys, and told them amusing stories. Now, Johnny delighted in these tales beyond any thing; so he and the old cowherd soon became

sworn friends. Among other things, Klas told
them many wonderful particulars about the dwarfs,
or little under-ground people, that dwelt within the
nine mountains. Of these dwarfs there are different

kinds, the white and the brown,—so called from the
colour of their clothes,—the former of which are
charming little elves, that are always friendly to the
human race. But only two of the mountains are
inhabited by these; the brown ones, that fill the

remaining mountains, are not exactly bad, but
wanton and tricksy. There were also black dwarfs,
who were wonderfully clever in all sorts of arts, and
excellent smiths, but deceitful and mischievous, and
not to be trusted; but none of these lived in that
neighbourhood. The dwarfs were fond of dancing in
the moonshine on a fine summer's night; and formerly
many a child was enticed by the sweet sound of their
music, which they mistook for birds, and were carried
away under ground by the little people, whom they
were condemned to serve for fifty years. At the end
of their time, the elves are obliged to give back all
their captives; and it is well for the latter that they
never become older than the age of twenty, even
though they had completed their half-century's du-
rance. All come back young and beautiful, and
generally meet with great luck in the world, either
because they have become wise and ingenious during
their stay below, or that the little people help them
unseen, and bring them gold and silver. But now-
a-days, said Klas, people had grown more cautious;
the spot was avoided; and it only seldom happened
that children were stolen. And in process of time,
too, as the old cowherd remarked, it had been found

out that, if any mortal was lucky enough to find or steal a cap belonging to one of the under-ground folk, he might go down in safety, and could not be detained against his will; and, so far from becoming their servant, the owner of the cap was obliged to do his bidding in every thing.

These wonderful tales had so fired little Johnny's imagination, that he thought of nothing but gold and silver cups, and glass shoes, and pockets full of ducats, and all the rest of the fine things described by the old cowherd as occasionally bestowed on their favourites by the dwarfs; and when midsummer came, and the nights were the shortest, he could resist no longer, but away he slunk after dark, and went and lay down on the top of the highest of the nine mountains, which Klas had informed him was their principal dancing-place. It must be confessed the little fellow felt some strange misgivings, and his heart thumped against his breast like a sledge-hammer; yet there he remained in breathless expectation from ten till twelve o'clock, at which hour he began to hear a rustling all around him, and the laughing, singing, and piping of innumerable little people, some of whom were dancing, and others playing a thousand merry antics. Johnny half shuddered as he heard them swarming about, (for he could not see them, as their caps made them invisible,) but he had sufficient presence of mind to lie perfectly quiet, and to pretend to be fast asleep, except that· he now and then stole

a glance, just to see if there was any chance of getting one of these diminutive beings into his power. Sure enough, before long three of the dwarfs approached the spot where he l·:y, though without perceiving him, and began to play at tossing their

110

caps up into the air, when one snatched his playmate's cap out of his hand in frolic sport, and flung
it away. The cap flew right over Johnny's face,
when he caught it softly, and, ringing the little
silver bell affixed to it in high glee, he put it on his
head, when he suddenly beheld the little subterranean people in countless thousands, they being now
no longer invisible to his sight. The three dwarfs
now came slily up to him to endeavour to snatch
back the cap, but the little boy held it fast, and they
saw that they should not succeed in that way, for
Johnny was a giant to them, as they only reached
to his knees. So the owner of the cap humbled himself before the finder, and begged him to restore his
property; but Johnny said, "You shall not get it,
you cunning little rogue. I should have fared badly
among you if I had not obtained some token of
yours; but, as it happens, you must do my bidding.
I have a fancy to go under ground and see what the
place is like, and you must be my servant, as you
well know." The little being pretended not to hear
or to understand, and continued whining most pite-
ously, till Johnny ordered him very imperiously to
bring him supper, as he was hungry. Away the

dwarf was obliged to scamper, and brought back bread, fruit, and wine, in a trice. And Johnny supped like a king, while he watched the games and the dancing of the little subterranean people.

When the cock had crowed three times, all was hushed in an instant, and nothing more was heard but hundreds of tiny feet tripping away to their respective mountains, which opened to receive them. On the top of the mountain where the ball had been held, and which but a moment before was covered with grass and flowers, there now rose a glass peak, which opened as each elf stepped upon it, and then closed again after they had slid down. As soon as all the inhabitants had entered, the peak disappeared entirely; while those who had fallen through the tube sank softly into a broad silver barrel, capable of holding a thousand such little folk as these, and which was fastened to silver chains that were drawn downwards and secured below. Johnny and his bondsman fell down with many others, and they all cried out to him to entreat him not to tread upon them, as his weight would kill them. He, however, took great care not to hurt any one. Several barrels were thus successively filled, till all had reached home.

Johnny was much surprised, on being let down, at the brightness of the walls, which seemed to be made of diamond; and when he was once below, he heard such lovely music that he was lulled immediately into a deep slumber.

When he woke, he felt as if he had slept a long while, and he found himself in the softest, neatest bed, such as he had never even seen before, which stood in the nicest chamber; while by his side stood his little brown elf, (for it was amongst the brown jackets that Johnny had fallen,) chasing away the flies with a feather fan, lest they should disturb his master's rest. Scarcely had Johnny opened his eyes, when his little valet brought him a basin and a towel,

and then an elegant suit of clothes, made of brown silk, and a pair of black shoes with red ties, far smarter than any Johnny had ever seen in Rambin or Rodenkirchen. Besides these, several pairs of the most beautiful glass shoes were laid by ready

114

to be worn on holidays. The little boy was vastly pleased to have such nice clothes given him, and was very willing to let himself be dressed. No sooner was his toilet completed, than the elf went and returned, on the wings of the wind, with a golden tray, bearing a bottle of sweet wine, a bowl of milk, fruit, bread, and a number of nice dishes, such as children are fond of. In short, a more obedient servant there could not be; a look from his master was enough without the help of words, for, like all the rest of the little people, the elf was wonderfully shrewd.

After breakfast, the dwarf opened a closet, in which were stowed away a number of bowls, chests, and vases containing gold and precious stones, while on another shelf stood a whole library of story-books filled with pretty pictures. Johnny was so well amused with looking at these, and admiring every thing around him, that he did not care to go out that morning. Indeed, the room itself might have excited the wonder even of those accustomed to a palace. Besides the snow-white bed with its satin pillows, there were curiously-carved chairs, inlaid with precious stones. Near the walls stood white marble tables, and a couple of smaller ones made of emerald; and at one end of the chamber were hung two looking-glasses set in jewelled frames. The walls of the chamber were wainscoted with table emeralds, and a large diamond ball was suspended from the

ceiling, and shed so bright a light that no other lamp was necessary. For it must be observed, that neither sun, moon, nor stars are to be seen under ground; nor is there any distinction between the seasons, which seems at first rather a drawback, but the temperature is always as mild as our spring, and the lustre of the precious stones supplies the place of daylight. Yet it is to be remarked that their days are never so bright, nor their nights so dark, as upon earth. So that all things have their compensation.

At noon a bell rang, when the serf cried, "Master, will you dine alone, or with the rest of the company?" "With the company," replied Johnny. The elf then led him forth, when Johnny, seeing nothing but a number of passages brilliantly lit up with precious stones, and little men and women, who popped out one by one, apparently from clefts in the rock, inquired where the company was. He had scarcely spoken, before the passage through which they were passing widened, and became an immense hall, with a large dome inlaid with diamonds, and Johnny perceived a countless throng of elegantly-dressed little men and women entering by a number of open doors, while tables loaded with delicious viands came up through the floor, and chairs arranged themselves ready for the guests. The principal personages now came to welcome Johnny, and placed him at table by the side of some of the loveliest maidens. The dinner was very gay, for the under-ground folks are

remarkably cheerful and frolicsome; and there was
the sweetest music all the time, proceeding from a
number of artificial birds, so cunningly made by
these clever little people that they sang and flew
about as though they had really belonged to the
feathered tribes that inhabit our woods. The elves
were waited upon by the boys and girls who had
fallen into their power from having come down
without previously securing a pledge; and it was
they who sprinkled the floor with perfumes, who
handed about the golden goblets, and presented
silver and crystal baskets full of fruits to the guests.
These youths and maidens were dressed in white,
with blue caps, silver girdles, and delicate glass
shoes, so that their steps could always be heard.
Johnny pitied them at first, till he saw how cheerful
and how rosy they looked, and then he reflected that
they were much better off than he used to be when
he drove the cows.

After the party had sat at the social board for a
couple of hours, the principal elf rang a bell, and the
tables and chairs disappeared, and laurels, palm-trees,
and orange-trees grew up in their stead, and the little
people fell to dancing, till about what we should call

four o'clock in the afternoon, when they slipped away
one by one, and went either to their work or to amuse
themselves in some other manner. At night, supper
was held just as merrily, after which the elves went
up out of their mountain, while Johnny laid himself
quietly in bed, after saying his prayers as usual.

Johnny led this life for many weeks, during which
he saw but little of the elves, except at dinner and at
supper, as each lived in his own little crystal house,
deep in the bosom of the mountain, which was transparent from one end to the other, though not to the
eyes of a mere child of earth. Yet occasionally he
met a stray elf hurrying along, when he was taking a
walk with his little serf. For he had found out there
were lakes, and fields, and trees, here below, just as
on the earth above; only there was a crystal vault
that invariably led from one meadow, or one lake,
into another district, though each patch of land or
sheet of water was sometimes a mile in circumference.
It was during one of these walks, after he had been
many months below, that Johnny once perceived a
snow-white figure, with long white locks, vanish
through a crystal wall in the rock; when he asked
his servant whether any of the elves were dressed in

white, like the youths and maids in waiting. The elf told him there were a few such, who were the oldest and most learned among them; that they were several thousand years old, and never appeared at table except once a year, on the birthday of the mountain king, nor left their chambers except to teach the children of the dwarfs and those of mortal birth, for whom there was a separate school. When Johnny heard this, he scolded his serving manikin for not having told him sooner that there was a school, and he ordered him to conduct him thither the next day, as he had a great wish to acquire some learning. So on the morrow Johnny went to school, where the children received excellent instruction in arts and sciences, besides being taught poetry and literature and different kinds of handicraft. Johnny soon grew to like his book better than any idle amusement, and acquired, besides, the art of drawing and painting, and grew so clever a goldsmith ·that he could imitate fruit and flowers in precious stones to admiration. And here Johnny found many play-mates, both among the boys and the girls, and spent several years very contentedly, until his education was quite completed.

120

Hans in Luck.

HANS had served his master for seven long years, when he said to him, "Master, my time is now up: so please to give me my wages, as I wish to return home to my mother." The master answered, "You have served me like a trusty, honest fellow, as you are; and such as your services have been, so shall be your hire."

And thereupon he gave him a piece of gold as large as Hans's head. Hans took a cloth and rolled up the lump of gold and slung it over his shoulder, and began to trudge home. As he went along, and kept setting one foot before the other, he happened to come up with a traveller, who was riding at a brisk pace on a lively horse.

"Oh, what a delightful thing it is to ride!" cried Hans, aloud: "it is every bit as good as sitting on a chair: one doesn't knock one's toes against a stone, and one saves one's shoes, and yet one gets on, one hardly knows how."

The man on horseback, having heard these wise

reflections, cried out to him, "Nay, then, Hans, why do you go on foot?"

"Why, you see, I am obliged to carry this lump home," replied Hans, "and, gold though it be, it bothers me sadly, as I am obliged to hold my head on one side, and it weighs so heavily on my shoulder."

"I'll tell you what," said the rider, stopping his horse: "we can make a bargain. Suppose I were to give you my horse, and you were to let me have your lump in exchange?"

"That I will, and thank you too," said Hans; "but I remind you that you will have to drag it along as best you may."

The traveller got down from his horse, and took the lump of gold, and then helped Hans to mount, and, having placed the bridle in his hand, said to him, "When you want to go very fast, you have only to smack your tongue and cry, 'Hop! hop!'"

Hans was in great delight, as he sat on the horse, and found he rode along so easily and so pleasantly. After a while, however, he fancied he should like to go a little quicker: so he began to smack his tongue and to shout, "Hop! hop!"

The horse set off at a brisk trot, and, before Hans had time to collect his thoughts, he was pitched into a ditch that divided the main road from the adjoining fields. The horse would have cleared the ditch at a

bound, had he not been stopped by a peasant, who was driving a cow along the same road, and happened to come up with the luckless rider just at this moment. Hans crawled out of the ditch as best he might, and got upon his legs again. But he was sorely vexed, and observed to the peasant that riding was no joke, especially when one had to do with a troublesome beast that thought nothing of kicking and plunging, and breaking a man's neck, and that nobody should ever catch him again attempting to mount such a dangerous animal. Then he concluded by saying, "How far preferable a creature is your cow! One can walk quietly behind her, let alone her furnishing you with milk, butter, and cheese, for certain, every day. What would I not give to have such a cow for my own!"

"Well," said the peasant, "if that's all, I should not mind changing my cow for your horse."

Hans agreed most joyfully to such a proposal, and the peasant leaped into the saddle and was presently out of sight.

Hans now drove the cow before him at a quiet pace, and kept ruminating upon the excellent bargain he had made. "If I have only a bit of bread,—and that is not likely to fail me,—I shall be able to add butter and cheese to it as often as I wish. If I feel thirsty, I need only milk my cow, and I shall have milk to drink."

124

On reaching a public house, he stopped to rest himself, and in the fulness of his joy he ate up his dinner and supper all at one meal, and spent his two remaining farthings to purchase half a glass of beer. He then went his way, and continued driving his cow towards his mother's village.

Towards noon, the heat grew more and more oppressive, particularly as Hans was crossing a moor during a full hour's time. At length his thirst became so intolerable that his tongue cleaved to the roof of his mouth. "The remedy is simple enough," thought Hans, "and now is the time to milk my cow and refresh myself with a good draught of milk."

He then tied his cow to the stump of a tree, and used his leather cap for a pail; but, do what he would, not a drop of milk could he obtain; and, as he set about attempting to milk the cow in the most awkward manner imaginable, the enraged animal gave him a hearty kick with her hind leg, that laid him sprawling on the ground, where he remained half stunned for a long time, and scarcely able to recollect where he was.

Fortunately, there just came by a butcher trundling a wheelbarrow, in which lay a young pig.

"What the deuce is the matter?" asked he, as he helped the worthy Hans to rise.

Hans related what had happened, when the butcher handed him his flask, saying, "There, man, take a draught, and it will soon bring you round again. The cow has no milk to give, for she is an old animal, only fit for the yoke, or to be killed and eaten."

126

"Lord, now! who would have thought it?" said Hans, stroking his hair over his forehead. "It is, to be sure, all very well to have such an animal as that to kill, particularly as it yields such a lot of meat; but then I don't much relish cow's flesh: it is not half juicy enough for me. I'd much rather have a young pig like yours. The flesh is far more tasty, to say nothing of the sausages."

"I'll tell you what, Hans," quoth the butcher, "I'll let you have my pig in exchange for your cow, just out of kindness."

"Now, that's very good of you, upon my word," replied Hans, as he gave him the cow, while the butcher took the pig out of the wheelbarrow, and put the string that was tied round the animal's leg into his new master's hand.

As Hans went along, he could not help marvelling at his constant run of luck, which had regularly turned every little disappointment to the very best account. After a time he was overtaken by a lad who was carrying a fine white goose under his arm. They no sooner bid one another good-morrow, than Hans related how lucky he had been, and what advantageous bargains he had struck. The lad told him, in turn, that he was carrying the goose to a christening-dinner. "Only just feel how heavy it is," continued he, taking the goose up by the wings;

"it has been fattening these eight weeks. I'll be bold to say that whoever tastes a slice of it when it comes to be roasted, will have to wipe away the fat from each corner of his mouth."

128

"Ay," said Hans, as he weighed it in one hand, "it is heavy enough, to be sure; but my pig is not to be sneezed at, either."

Meanwhile the lad was looking all around him with an anxious air, and then shook his head as he observed, " It's my mind your pig will get you into trouble. I have just come through a village where the mayor's pig was stolen out of its sty, and I'm mightily afraid it's the very pig you are now driving. It would be a bad job for you if you were caught with it, and the least that could happen to you would be a lodging in the black hole."

Poor Hans now began to be frightened. "For goodness' sake," cried he, "do help me out of this scrape; and, as you know this neighbourhood better than I do, pray take my pig in exchange for your goose."

"I know I shall run some risk," replied the lad; "yet I haven't the heart to leave you in the lurch, either."

And, so saying, he took hold of the rope, and drove away the pig as fast as he could into a by-way, while honest Hans pursued his road with the goose under his arm.

129

"When I come to think of it," said he to himself,
"I have gained by the exchange. In the first place,
a nice roast goose is a delicious morsel; then there

will be the fat and the dripping to spread upon our
bread for months to come; and, last of all, the beautiful white feathers will serve to fill my pillow, and

130

I'll warrant I shall not want rocking to sleep. How pleased my mother will be!"

As he passed through the last village on his way home, he saw a knife-grinder busily turning his wheel, while he kept singing,—

"Old knives and old scissors to make new I grind,
And round turns my wheel e'en as swift as the wind."

Hans stopped to look at him, and at last he said, "Your trade must be a good one, since you sing so merrily over your work."

"Yes," replied the knife-grinder, "it is a golden business. Your true knife-grinder is a man who finds money as often as he puts his hand into his pocket. But where did you buy that fine goose?" "I did not buy it, but exchanged it for my pig." "And where did you get piggy from?" "I swapped my cow for it." "And how did you come by your cow?" "Oh, I gave a horse for it." "And how might you have obtained the horse?" "Why, I got it in exchange for a lump of gold as big as my head." "And how did you come by the gold?" "It was my wages for seven years' service." "Nay, then," said the knife-

131

grinder, " since you have been so clever each time, you need only manage so as to hear the money jingle in your pocket every time you move, and then you will be a made man." " But how shall I set about that?" inquired Hans. " You must turn knife-grinder like myself; and nothing is wanting to set you up in the trade but a grindstone: the rest will come of itself. I have one here that is a trifle worn, but I won't ask for any thing more than your goose in exchange for it. Shall it be a bargain?" " How can you doubt it?" replied Hans: " I shall be the happiest man on earth. Why, if I find money as often as I put my hand in my pocket, what more need I care for?" And he handed him the goose, and took the grindstone. " Now," said the knife-grinder, picking up a tolerably heavy stone that lay on the ground by him, " here's a good solid stone into the bargain, on which you can hammer away, and straighten all your old crooked nails. You had better lay it on the top of the other."

Hans did so, and went away quite delighted. " I was surely born with a golden spoon in my mouth," cried he, while his eyes sparkled with joy, " for every thing falls out just as pat as if I were a Sunday child." In the mean time, however, having walked since daybreak, he now began to feel tired and very hungry, as he had eaten up all his provisions in his joy at the bargain he had made for the cow. By degrees he could scarcely drag his weary limbs any farther, and was obliged to stop every minute to rest from the fatigue of carrying the two heavy stones. At length he could not help thinking how much better it would be if he had not to carry them at all. He had now crawled like a snail up to a spring, where he meant to rest, and refresh himself with a cool draught; and for this purpose he placed the stones very carefully on the brink of the well. He then sat down, and was stooping over the well to drink, when he happened to push the stones inadvertently, and plump into the water they fell! Hans no sooner saw them sink to the bottom of the well, than he got up joyfully, and then knelt down to thank Heaven for having thus mercifully ridded him of his heavy burden without the slightest reproach on his own conscience. For these stones were the only things that stood in his way. "There is not a luckier fellow than I beneath the sun," exclaimed Hans; and, with a light heart and empty

hands, he now bounded along till he reached his mother's home.

Jack the Giant-Killer.

In the reign of King Arthur, there lived near the Land's End, in the county of Cornwall, an honest farmer, whose son Jack was a bold boy, who delighted in reading stories about wizards, giants, and fairies, and listened eagerly whenever anybody related the brave deeds of the Knights of the Round Table. Jack was fond of planning sieges and battles, and raising mimic ramparts, while tending the cattle in the fields; and as to wrestling, there were few or none equal to him, even among boys older than himself. So Jack thought he was a match for a giant who dwelt in a cavern on the top of St. Michael's Mount, and who for years had ravaged the coast, carrying off half a dozen oxen at a time on his back, and three times as many sheep and hogs round his waist. Still, little as Jack was, compared to such an adversary, he resolved to rid the country of such a nuisance, and, setting off one evening, with a horn, a pickaxe, and a dark lantern, he swam to the mount, at the foot of which he dug a deep pit before morning; this he covered with sticks and straw, and having strewed it with earth,

135

so as to look like solid ground, he blew a loud blast on his horn which awoke the giant. "You saucy villain," roared the monster, "you shall pay dearly for disturbing my rest: I will broil you for my breakfast."

So saying, out came the giant with tremendous strides, when, lo! he tumbled right into the pit; and, before he could recover himself, Jack clove his skull with his pickaxe. The justices of Cornwall, on hearing of so bold a deed, sent for Jack, and, telling him he should henceforth be called JACK the GIANT-KILLER, presented him with a sword and belt on which was engraved, in golden letters,—

"This is the valiant Cornish man
That slew the giant Cormoran."

The fame of Jack's exploit soon spread throughout the west of England, when another giant, called old Blunderbore, who inhabited an enchanted castle in the midst of a wood, vowed he would avenge his brother giant, if ever he should get the audacious stripling in his power. Now, four months after Cormoran's death, Jack took a journey into Wales, and passed through this very wood; when, having fallen asleep by the side of a fountain, the giant

136

found him on coming to draw water, and, seeing who he was from the lines on his belt, he laid him gently on his shoulder and carried him off to his castle.

On reaching the castle, he found the floor covered with the skulls and bones of human beings, and the giant told him, with a horrid grin, that men's hearts eaten with pepper and vinegar were his tit-bits, and that he hoped to make a dainty meal on his heart. So saying, he locked Jack up, and went to invite another giant to dine with him. No sooner was he gone than Jack heard dreadful shrieks from several parts of the castle, while a mournful voice urged him to fly before the giant returned with another more savage than himself. Poor Jack was ready to go mad on hearing these words; and, running to the window, he saw the two giants coming along arm in arm. Luckily, there were two stout cords in the room, and Jack lost no time in making a noose at the end of each, and as the two giants entered the gates, which were under the window, he threw the ropes over their heads, and fastening the ends to a beam in the ceiling, he pulled and pulled till both were black in the face, and then, sliding down with the help of the cords, he drew his sword and killed them. Jack next took a bunch of keys from Blunderbore's pocket, and, on searching the castle, found three poor ladies tied up by their hair, and nearly starved to death. So

Jack kindly gave them the castle and all it contained, and proceeded on his journey to Wales.

By the time night had come on, Jack had reached

138

a lonely valley, where he discovered a large, handsome house. Having knocked at the gate, Jack
was rather alarmed at being answered by a monstrous giant with two heads, but with only one eye
to each head. However, he spoke very civilly,
and no sooner had Jack told him he had lost his
way, than he welcomed him to his house, and
showed him into a room, where he found a very
good bed. Jack undressed himself, but could not
get a wink of sleep; and presently he heard the
giant in the next room, muttering to himself,—

"Though you lodge with me this night,
You shall not see the morning light;
My club shall dash your brains out quite."

Hearing this, Jack got out of bed, and groped
about the room till he found a thick log of wood,
which he laid in the bed, while he hid himself in a
corner of the room. In the middle of the night
the giant came, and struck so many blows on the
bed that he thought he had broken all Jack's
bones. So we may fancy his surprise when his
guest entered his room next morning, to thank him
for his lodging.

"Dear me!" stammered the giant, "is it you?

139

and pray how did you sleep? Did nothing disturb you in the middle of the night?"

"Nothing worth mentioning," replied Jack, carelessly; "I believe a rat just flapped me three or four times with his tail, but I soon went to sleep again."

The giant was very much surprised, but he said nothing, and went to fetch two large bowls of hasty pudding for breakfast. Jack now thought it would be a good joke to make the giant believe he could

140

eat as much as himself; so he slipped the pudding into a leathern bag inside his coat, while he made believe to put it into his mouth. When breakfast was over, he said, "Now I will show you a trick." So saying, he took a knife and ripped up the bag, when all the hasty pudding fell out upon the floor. "Ods splutter hur nails!" cried the Welsh giant, "hur can do that hurself." So he plunged the knife into his stomach, and dropped dead.

Jack continued his journey, and a few days after fell in with King Arthur's only son, who had travelled to Wales to deliver a beautiful lady from the power of a wicked magician. When Jack found that the prince had no attendants with him, he offered his services, which were thankfully accepted. The prince was so kind-hearted that he gave away his money to every one he met; and, having parted with his last penny, he asked Jack what they should do to get food and lodging for that night. Jack begged him to leave that to him, for that two miles farther on there lived a giant with three heads, who could fight five hundred men. The prince feeling uneasy at the idea of claiming the hospitality of such a monster, Jack told him to stay behind, and he would manage him. Accordingly, on Jack rode, and knocked at the castle-gate. "Who is there?" thundered out the giant. "Only your poor cousin Jack," said our hero. "Well, what news, cousin Jack?" asked the giant. "Bad news, dear uncle," quoth Jack. "Pooh!" answered the giant: "what can be bad news for me, who have three heads, and can fight five hundred men?" "Alas!" said Jack, "the king's son is coming with two thousand men, to kill you and destroy your castle." "This is bad news indeed, cousin Jack," cried the giant; "but I will hide myself in the cellar, and you shall lock me in, and keep the key till the king's son is gone."

In the morning, when the prince had gone, Jack let out the giant, who, as a reward for saving his castle, gave our hero a coat which made its wearer invisible, a cap which imparted knowledge, a sword which could cut through every thing, and shoes which lent a marvellous swiftness to the feet.

Jack thanked the giant many times, and then joined the prince. They soon reached the castle where the beautiful lady was kept in thraldom by the wicked magician, and here Jack learned, by putting on his cap of knowledge, that the wizard

142

went every night into the forest to conjure up spirits: so he dressed himself in the coat of darkness, and, drawing on his shoes of swiftness, ran after him and cut off his head, which ended the enchantment and set the lady free. The prince married her the next day, and the royal pair proceeded with their deliverer to the court of King Arthur, who was so pleased with his prowess that he made him a knight of the Round Table.

Jack begged the king to equip him, that he might return to Wales and rid his majesty's subjects of all the remaining giants. To this King Arthur consented, and accordingly Jack took his leave of the court, and after travelling for three days reached a forest, which he had no sooner entered than he heard most dreadful shrieks, and on peeping through the trees he perceived a monstrous giant dragging along by their hair a handsome knight and his beautiful lady. Jack immediately alighted from his horse, and put on his invisible coat, under which he carried his sword of sharpness, and approaching the giant, who was so tall that he could not reach his body, he wounded him so severely on his knee that the huge monster fell to the ground, when Jack

143

at once cut off his head. The knight and his lady
now approached, and, thanking him most heartily,
entreated him to come and rest himself at their

house. "No," said Jack, "I cannot rest till I find
out the den the monster inhabited."

On hearing this, the knight grew very sorrowful,
and told him that it was too much to risk his life a
second time, for that the giant lived in a den under

a neighbouring mountain, with a brother yet fiercer and more cruel than himself. But our valiant giant-killer was not to be put off his purpose so easily, so straightway he mounted his horse and rode off.

After riding a mile and a half, he came in sight of the mouth of the cavern, and saw the giant seated on a block of timber with a club by his side. Jack got down from his horse, and, putting on his coat of darkness, said, "So, here is the other monster: I'll soon pluck him by the beard." He then struck a blow at his head, but missed his aim, and the giant, feeling wounded, yet seeing no one near, began to lay about him with his club. Jack, however, slipped nimbly behind him and quickly cut off his head, and sent it, together with that of his brother, to King Arthur.

Next day Jack set out for the knight's house, where he was welcomed with great joy and feasting. When the company were assembled, the knight related to them the Giant-Killer's exploits, and then presented Jack with a handsome ring, on which was engraved the picture of the giant dragging along the hapless couple.

In the midst of the festivities a messenger rushed

in with the news that Thundel, a giant with two heads, was coming to avenge the death of his kinsmen. Jack immediately set some men to cut the drawbridge, that lay across the moat, almost to the

middle, and, having put on his coat of darkness, he sallied forth to meet the giant.

Though the giant could not see him, he sniffed his presence, and cried out,—

150

JACK THE GIANT-KILLER.

"Fee! foh! fum!
I smell the blood of an Englishman:
Be he alive, or be he dead,
I'll grind his bones to make me bread."

"You must catch me first," said Jack, and, flinging off his coat and putting on his shoes, he began to run, the giant following him like a walking castle. Jack led him round and round the moat, that the company might see him, and then ran over the drawbridge; but when the giant, still pursuing him, came to the middle where the bridge had been cut, his weight snapped it at once, and he fell into the water. Jack then called for a rope, and, throwing a noose over his double neck, he drew him to the edge of the moat, and cut off his heads, which he likewise despatched to King Arthur.

Jack then set out in search of new adventures, and at last reached the foot of a high mountain. Here he lodged for the night at the house of an old hermit, who, recognizing him as the famous Giant-Killer, told him that at the top of the mountain there was an enchanted castle, kept by a giant, who by the help of a wicked magician detained a number of knights and ladies whom he had changed

147

into beasts; and, among the rest, a duke's daughter, whom they had seized in her father's garden, and brought through the air in a chariot drawn by two fiery dragons, and then turned into a deer. "Many knights have tried to destroy the enchantment," added the hermit, "but none have succeeded, on account of two fiery griffins; but you, my son, have an invisible coat, and can therefore pass them."

Jack promised he would do all that lay in his power to break the enchantment, and, rising early next morning, he put on his invisible coat, and, climbing to the top of the mountain, passed between the fiery griffins, when he found a golden trumpet on the castle-gate, under which was written,—

"Whoever can this trumpet blow
Shall cause the giant's overthrow."

Jack then seized the trumpet and blew a shrill blast, which made the gates fly open and the very castle tremble, while the giant and conjurer, knowing their wicked course was at an end, stood biting their thumbs and shaking with fear. Jack killed the giant with his sword of sharpness, the magician was carried off by a whirlwind, and all the knights and ladies returned to their proper shapes, and the castle vanished like smoke. The whole party then set out for the court, and when King Arthur heard the account of Jack's noble deeds, he begged the duke to give him his daughter in marriage, and then presented him with a fine estate, on which the young couple lived for the rest of their days in peace and happiness.

The House That Jack Built.

This is the malt,
That lay in the house that Jack built.

This is the rat,

That ate the malt,

That lay in the house that Jack built.

151

This is the cat,
That kill'd the rat,
That ate the malt,
That lay in the house that Jack built.

THE HOUSE THAT JACK BUILT.

This is the dog,
That worried the cat,
That kill'd the rat,
That ate the malt,
That lay in the house that Jack built.

This is the cow with the crumpled horn,
 That toss'd the dog,
 That worried the cat,
 That kill'd the rat,
 That ate the malt,
That lay in the house that Jack built.

154

THE HOUSE THAT JACK BUILT.

This is the maiden all forlorn,
That milk'd the cow with the crumpled horn,
      That toss'd the dog,
      That worried the cat,
      That kill'd the rat,
      That ate the malt,
That lay in the house that Jack built.

THE HOUSE THAT JACK BUILT.

This is the man all tatter'd and torn,
That kiss'd the maiden all forlorn,
That milk'd the cow with the crumpled horn,
  That toss'd the dog,
  That worried the cat,
  That killed the rat,
  That ate the malt,
That lay in the house that Jack built.

THE HOUSE THAT JACK BUILT.

This is the priest all shaven and shorn,
That married the man all tatter'd and torn,
That kiss'd the maiden all forlorn,
That milk'd the cow with the crumpled horn,
     That toss'd the dog,
     That worried the cat,
     That kill'd the rat,
     That ate the malt,
That lay in the house that Jack built.

THE HOUSE THAT JACK BUILT.

THE HOUSE THAT JACK BUILT.

This is the cock that crow'd in the morn,
That waked the priest all shaven and shorn,
That married the man all tatter'd and torn,
That kiss'd the maiden all forlorn,
That milk'd the cow with the crumpled horn,
   That toss'd the dog,
   That worried the cat,
   That kill'd the rat,
   That ate the malt,
That lay in the house that Jack built.

THE HOUSE THAT JACK BUILT.

THE HOUSE THAT JACK BUILT.

This is the farmer who sow'd the corn,
That kept the cock that crow'd in the morn,
That waked the priest all shaven and shorn,
That married the man all tatter'd and torn,
That kiss'd the maiden all forlorn,
That milk'd the cow with the crumpled horn,
  That toss'd the dog,
  That worried the cat,
  That kill'd the rat,
  That eat the malt,
That lay in the house that Jack built.

THE HOUSE THAT JACK BUILT.

162

THE HOUSE THAT JACK BUILT.

This is the horse, and the hound, and the horn,
That belong'd to the farmer who sow'd the corn,
That kept the cock that crow'd in the morn,
That awaked the priest all shaven and shorn,
That married the man all tatter'd and torn,
That kiss'd the maiden all forlorn,
That milk'd the cow with the crumpled horn,
   That toss'd the dog,
   That worried the cat,
   That kill'd the rat,
   That ate the malt,
That lay in the house that Jack built.

Little Bo-Peep.

LITTLE Bo-peep has lost her sheep,
    And cannot tell where to find 'em:
Leave them alone, and they'll come home,
    And bring their tails behind 'em.

LITTLE BO-PEEP.

Little Bo-peep fell fast asleep,
  And dreamt she heard them bleating:
When she awoke, she found it a joke,
  For still they all were fleeting.

Then up she took her little crook,
  Determined for to find them:
She found them indeed, but it made her heart bleed,
  For they'd left their tails behind them.

It happen'd one day, as Bo-peep did stray
  Into a meadow hard by,
There she espied their tails side by side,
  All hung on a tree to dry.

LITTLE BO-PEEP.

She heaved a sigh, and wiped her eye,
    And over the hillocks she raced;
And tried what she could, as a shepherdess should,
    That each tail should be properly placed.

166

The Old Woman and her Eggs.

THERE was an old woman, as I've heard tell,
She went to the market her eggs for to sell:
She went to the market, all on a market-day,
And she fell asleep on the king's highway.

THE OLD WOMAN AND HER EGGS.

There came a little peddler,—his name it was Stout:
He cut off her petticoats all round about:
He cut off her petticoats up to her knees,
Until her poor knees began for to freeze.

When the little woman began to awake,
She began to shiver and she began to shake:
Her knees began to freeze and she began to cry,
"Oh, lawk! oh, mercy on me! this surely can't be I.

"If it be not I, as I suppose it be,
I have a little dog at home, and he knows me:
If it be I, he will wag his little tail;
But if it be not I he'll bark and he'll rail."

Up jump'd the little woman, all in the dark;
Up jump'd the little dog, and he began to bark:
The dog began to bark, and she began to cry,
"Oh, lawk! oh, mercy on me! I see it is not I.'

15   **169**

Old Mother Goose.

OLD Mother Goose, when
She wanted to wander,
Would ride through the air
On a very fine gander.

Mother Goose had a house:
　'Twas built in the wood,
Where an owl at the door
　For a sentinel stood.

This is her son Jack,—
　A plain-looking lad:
He is not very good,
　Nor yet very bad.

She sent him to market:
　A live goose he bought:
" Here, mother," says he,
　" It will not go for naught."

OLD MOTHER GOOSE.

Jack's goose and her gander
   Grew very fond:
They'd both eat together,
   Or swim in one pond.

Jack found one morning,
   As I have been told,
His goose had laid him
   An egg of pure gold.

Jack rode to his mother,
   The news for to tell:
She call'd him a good boy,
   And said it was well.

OLD MOTHER GOOSE.

Jack sold his gold egg
  To a rogue of a Jew,
Who cheated him out of
  The half of his due.

Then Jack went a-courting
  A lady so gay,
As fair as the lily,
  And sweet as the May.

The Jew and the Squire
  Came close at his back,
And began to belabour
  The sides of poor Jack.

15*

They threw the gold egg
In the midst of the sea;
But Jack he jump'd in,
And got it back presently.

The Jew got the goose,
Which he vow'd he would kill,
Resolving at once
His pockets to fill.

Jack's mother came in,
And caught the goose soon,
And, mounting its back,
Flew up to the moon.

Dance, little baby, dance up high:
Never mind, baby, mother is nigh:
Crow and caper, caper and crow:
There, little baby, there you go,
Up to the ceiling, down to the ground,
Backward and forward, round and round.